THE AMISH GIRL WHO NEVER BELONGED (AMISH ROMANCE)

AMISH MISFITS BOOK 1

SAMANTHA PRICE

CHAPTER 1

The cold air blew in through the slight opening of Emma's bedroom window. Goosebumps broke out on her skin, causing her to shiver in the morning breeze. Remembering that today was her birthday, she pulled her blankets around her neck. A birthday would be a happy occasion to anyone else, but birthdays had never been that way for Emma, not for a long time.

Burying her head in the pillow, she thought back to her seventh birthday.

She was the only child at her parents' funeral; that was one thing she noticed.

Emma stood right by the graves as the tall men lowered the coffins into the ground.

"Come here, Emma!"

Emma knew her grandmother was calling her but chose to ignore her. She knew what death was even at that young age. She'd had the family dog die, and some of the farm animals had died, for one reason or another.

Her parents were gone for good and not coming back. It was final.

"Emma." Once again, the shrill voice rang through the cold air.

After ignoring the older woman one more time, Emma was pulled off balance when her hand was grabbed.

Screaming for all she was worth, Emma pulled out of her grandmother's grasp and stomped her black boots into the grass.

Nothing and no one would prevent her

from seeing her parents' funeral through to the end.

She was going to be close to them for as long as she possibly could.

Once the coffins were in the ground, the two teams of men slid the ropes out from beneath them, took up shovels, and began to fill the graves. Each shovelful of dirt that landed on the coffins echoed through her head and her heart.

Emma stood still and watched in pain—a pain that was too deep for tears.

From behind her, she heard her grandmother talking.

"She is uncontrollable. I don't know what I'll do with her."

"You don't have to deal with her, Bessie. You're too old to worry about young children. I'm sure another family will take her."

"Who would take her once they realize she's uncontrollable and foul-tempered?"

"I'll ask around for you, but I think you're right. She's not going to change her ways."

"My son has spoiled her, but it was Ida who swayed him to do so."

Now her grandmother was being mean about her mother. *Mamm* had never really gotten along with her mother-in-law. Sure, they were polite on the surface, but there were always ripples of tension when her grandmother was nearby.

"Emma! It's getting cold, and everyone's left."

Emma said a silent goodbye to her parents and hoped the bishop was right and she would see them again one day. "I'm coming." She walked to the waiting buggy and climbed in.

Then, to the sound of clip-clopping of hooves, she looked back at the graves until they were out of sight.

Once they were close to her grandmother's house, her grandmother told her, "Don't think you can act the same way you always have. There are going to be some changes whether you like it or not."

Emma looked at the fields they were passing. "Good. I like changes."

"You're not going to like these ones."

"I think I will."

"You're defiant. You must have the devil in you. Your will must be broken."

Emma had no idea what she meant by that. What she did know was that she and her grandmother were opposites, like night and day, or black and white.

No matter what Emma did, her grandmother thought the worst of her.

DESPITE SEVERAL ATTEMPTS her grandmother made to have her live with someone else, it wasn't until she was eleven that she went to help Mrs. Esh care for her family. She had two stints living with them.

At seventeen, she came to live with Joseph and Molly Schwartz—her only living relatives now that her grandmother had died.

Joseph was a cousin to her father, and they had the same last name as she, which gave her a sense of belonging. The best thing was that Joseph and Molly Schwartz had a daughter nearly Emma's age—just two years younger.

Aunt Molly was a nice, caring woman, but she was the kind of *fraa* to follow her husband's orders with no question; something that Emma didn't agree with in the slightest. Still, her aunt and uncle, as she called them even though they were cousins of some degree, had taken her in when she'd had nowhere to go. After the hardships she'd faced, life with Joseph, Molly, and their daughter, Katie, was now pleasant. Nevertheless, each birthday still filled her with dread.

Knowing that her twentieth birthday couldn't be as bad as her seventh, or as bad as her seventeenth when she'd been forced to leave the comfort of Mrs. Esh's house after she died, Emma rolled out of bed, dressed, and headed to the kitchen.

It was somewhat of a tradition in their home, as many things were, to sit together for breakfast every morning. Katie sometimes slept in and avoided it, but Emma had no such luxury. The one time she had overslept and completely missed breakfast, *Onkel* Joseph had given her the cold shoulder for the entire day. Since then, she had made sure to never again ignore tradition in that house.

"Good morning," Uncle Joseph said, flashing a bright smile as she walked in. "Happy Birthday."

"*Denke, Onkel,*" she said, taking her usual seat at the table.

"I made your favorite," Aunt Molly said,

placing a plate of pancakes and maple syrup in front of her.

"*Wunderbaar, denke.* It looks so tasty."

"Katie is still asleep, but she should be down soon. She's been very excited about your birthday." Aunt Molly sat down at the table.

"Me too," Emma said, not wanting to share her fear of something bad happening.

Emma's thoughts drifted away, back to when she used to make breakfast pancakes for the Esh boys. Her grandmother thought hard work would bring her into line and had sent her off at eleven to help Mrs. Esh run her household.

Mrs. Esh was a kindly woman but mostly bedridden. Her six boys were all full-grown and rowdy. Emma cooked them three meals a day. Not only that, she'd do all of their mending and washing, and clean the house. She felt like an unpaid servant, a slave, but then at night she would slip into Mrs. Esh's warm bed and while they drank hot tea, Mrs. Esh taught her to read. Emma was there for two years until Mrs. Esh regained strength and then Emma was sent back to her grandmother.

"How is it?"

Emma was jolted out of her daydreams when her aunt spoke. "Truly delicious," she said with a smile.

As her uncle talked to his wife about something he wanted her to do, Emma's mind drifted back to where she'd left her daydreams.

When she got back to her grandmother's house after her first stay with the Eshes, she lived there for the next year. Her grandmother was just the same as always, and days after Emma's arrival, she tried to send her to live with a different family.

Emma had refused.

Things had worked well with the Eshes and they'd been nice to her, but things could've been very different. Emma smiled when she remembered the Esh boys, but that jerked a distasteful memory of her grandmother into her mind.

"Now that you finished with the Eshes, I found another family that can use your help," her grandmother had said.

"Why can't I just stay here?" Emma had asked.

"Idle hands are the devil's playground."

"I don't know what that means."

"*Gott* says it's best to keep busy."

"Did He say that to you?"

"Don't try to be funny, girl."

"I'm not trying to be funny but I hear that a lot. *Gott* says this, or *Gott* says that. He's never said anything to me."

"When you get older, you'll know what He says because you'll read it in your Bible. But no, that's right, you're not bright enough to read."

Emma kept to herself that Mrs. Esh had

taught her to read. "I could learn to read if you would send me to school."

"School is a waste of time for a girl. You'll get married and all you will need to know is how to cook and clean and bear the children. Unless, like me, you only have one child before your husband goes to be with *Gott.*"

"When did my *grossdaddi* die?"

"Right after your *vadder* was born."

She looked so miserable that Emma had to ask, "Is that why you're always so cranky?"

Her grandmother's mouth formed a thin line before her mouth turned downwards at the corners while her green eyes narrowed. "That's a nasty thing to say."

"I didn't mean it to be nasty. I just thought that might be the reason, that's all."

"Tomorrow I'm sending you to the Gingerichs' and you can help them at their orchard."

"*Nee,* I don't want to. It sounds like hard work. I'd have to pick all the apples off the tree, or bend over and pick them all up and put them into buckets. The buckets will become heavy and I'm only a young girl. I won't be put to work like a man. *Nee!* I won't do it. I won't."

"You'll do as I say."

"*Nee.* I won't! You're not my *mudder* and you're so mean you probably killed your own husband just so I wouldn't have a *grossdaddi.*"

Emma thought the old woman might lash out and try to hit her. She hadn't meant to say something so horrid, but she was unhappy living with someone so wretched all the time. Everyone else in the community was happy except for her grandmother and a couple of her old friends.

"Go to your room! You're going to get the stick for that."

Emma turned and ran up the stairs and into her room, closing the door. Then she pushed her bed across the door so her grandmother couldn't get in.

Then Emma looked out the window and wondered if she should run away, but where would she go and how would she get food? At least at her grandmother's house she had shelter and food.

A few minutes later, her grandmother tried to open the door. "What have you done to the door?"

"I'm not letting you in if you're going to hit me. I'm sorry I said that you killed your husband. I didn't really mean it because I don't think you'd kill someone."

And then there was silence. It was only afternoon, but Emma crawled into bed, not game to go out and face her grandmother for the rest of the day.

The next day, nothing was said and there was no more talk of sending her to the Gingerichs' orchard. Somehow she'd escaped the stick, too. Maybe because she apologized; she was careful after that, not to upset her grandmother again.

CHAPTER 2

Emma pushed her grandmother out of her mind as she remembered the Esh boys once again. Phillip was the oldest, the bossy one who was always playing jokes and pranks on the others.

James, the second oldest, was the serious one who always tried to make the others behave. He tried to take the role as the father, but the other boys would have none of it.

Then there was Thomas, the third oldest, and Emma guessed him to be around nineteen or twenty back then. The rumors were he was a drunkard and a gambler. Emma had often found empty rum bottles behind the barn, covered over by the long grass. Word was, he got a girl from town into trouble, but that was swept under the rug, as many things were back then. Emma never heard much more about the scandal apart from the occasional whisper.

Michael was next in line, and then Isaiah. The youngest brother, David, was already earning himself a reputation as a very good furniture maker even though only in his middle-teens.

Even though the boys weren't around much except at mealtimes, they all helped when they were there. Not one of them sat back and left the work to Emma and she appreciated that. Best of all, though, she liked the nights with Mrs. Esh when they'd read and drink hot tea.

Emma was only back with her grandmother for a year when Mrs. Esh called for her again. She stayed with the Eshes for another year and then received word that her grandmother had died.

Then she found out the distressing news that her grandmother had left her money and her house to a relative Emma had never met, even though Emma's parents had willed their money to her grandmother to hold in trust for Emma, with the understanding that she use only what was needed for Emma's clothes and other necessities. Instead, her grandmother had left Emma penniless and feeling utterly alone.

She knew her parents would be upset that she had been left homeless and destitute.

Mrs. Esh said she must turn to *Gott* and that He had a home for her in heaven. When that did nothing to make Emma smile, Mrs. Esh told her she had a home there with them for the rest of her days.

Another year on, though, and Mrs. Esh

finally died after she could no longer fight her battle against cancer. She refused to go to the hospital, and in the end, refused any treatment at all.

The bishop told Emma it wasn't right that she live in a household of men who were not related to her, and that was when he tracked down Joseph Schwartz in a neighboring community.

Emma reminded herself to be grateful she had a home, a roof over her head and people who cared for her. She glanced at the table in front of her. There was even a fresh glass of milk. *"Denke* so much, both of you, for this lovely breakfast."

"Well, it's your birthday, and it's not any usual one. Now that you're getting older, we need to help you plan for the future. I think you should take a look at this and consider it," her uncle said, picking up a wrinkled newspaper from the chair next to him and handing it to her.

The paper crumpled in her hands, wrinkling even further. Within seconds, Emma knew what this meant. These were wedding announcements, and she knew that they wanted her to marry. Perhaps at twenty, she'd finally outstayed her welcome. "What is this for?"

"I think you know what it's for, dear," her aunt said, her smile quickly fading into a frown. "It's time you ... You have no job and nothing ... no direction—"

"What your aunt is saying is that you're at the age where you should be thinking of marriage. Well, to be clear, you're past the age. This is something we'd hoped you'd think of by yourself."

"But... but I don't want to get married—not yet," Emma said, still shaking her head. Marriage was something that she had never considered to be for herself. She didn't really know what love was, she was only used to having to accept loss and deal with the grief associated with it. Her aunt and uncle had loved her as much as they could over the past few years, but nothing could fill the hole that had been gouged into her heart when she was seven years old.

Now, she was deathly afraid that anyone she loved or cared about would also abandon her. She'd come to love Mrs. Esh and she'd been taken away.

"I can understand that, Emma, but we don't always have a choice in life. You're at the age now where finding a suitable husband will determine the quality of your days to come. Don't you want to start a *familye* and have your own *haus?*" Uncle Joseph's eyes focused on hers.

Emma gulped. She'd hoped this birthday would break the cycle of bad happenings, but that wasn't to be.

"I have you both, and Katie. I don't need a husband."

"Unfortunately, that is not the truth," he

said, sighing loudly. "I had a feeling that you wouldn't be too welcoming of the idea, but it's something beyond my control. You need to accept the responsibilities that come with age." He shook his head. "Twenty is well past the age for you to be thinking of marriage. Soon, Katie will be moving out of the *haus* when she gets married and that could be anytime now."

Emma opened her mouth, but stopped herself just in time. Mrs. Esh had taught her to hold her tongue when she wanted to make her point, and to think first before she spoke.

She'd been about to point out Katie didn't even have a young man in mind. "I know that I need to think about my future, but marrying me off to some man won't make my life good. I want to be free to explore my own options and do as I see fit. I thought that was what adults did." Her tone, even though she'd controlled it, quickly roused her uncle.

Uncle Joseph puffed out his chest. "Listen, I know this seems like it came out of nowhere, but the matter is not up for discussion and is now beyond my control. In fact, I've already had your aunt write to some families on your behalf."

Swiftly her gaze moved to Aunt Molly. Her aunt's gaze dropped to the table and she remained silent. Aunt Molly would've known she didn't want this. She'd talked with her aunt and Katie of wanting to be a teacher, or perhaps to help young ones who were struggling with learning to read. Now all choice had been taken from her.

In a state of disbelief, Emma sat there. Uncle Joseph would never have done that to Katie.

Her birthday was now officially ruined— as she had known it would be— and without saying anything else on the matter, she excused herself from the table.

Her aunt looked troubled. "You haven't even—"

"Let her go, Molly," she heard Uncle Joseph say just as she was halfway out of the kitchen.

CHAPTER 3

One by one, she walked up the wooden stairs to her bedroom. This place had been her home for the last few years, but what they'd done to her this morning was a stark reminder that it wasn't truly her home.

Feeling unwanted again, she lay down on her bed. Even though all she wanted to do was cry, she couldn't force a tear.

Life hadn't been all bad.

Sure, it had been bad with her grandmother who rarely smiled or said a kind word, but the Eshes had all been nice to her. Even though she was out of place in a houseful of boys and didn't feel as though she fit in, maybe that was the only place she had belonged after her parents had died. The kindness Mrs. Esh had shown her, reminded her of the vague memories of her mother.

Emma groaned loudly and heard her voice reverberate around the bare walls of the sparsely furnished room. What would her life have been like had her parents' buggy not been hit by the runaway truck that'd lost its brakes? The police had found her in the back of the buggy while her parents had been thrown clear.

Even though she'd not seen her parents' bodies as they lay lifeless on the ground, she knew that something bad had happened and had screamed for all she was worth when they pulled her from the buggy. The buggy was dark and safe—what was outside was unknown.

After another huge sigh, she was free of those memories and back on her bed, and, as Mrs. Esh had told her to do whenever she felt unfairly treated, she put herself in her aunt and uncle's place.

From their point of view, she guessed they were being mindful of her future because she couldn't stay living there forever—she wasn't their child.

Emma bit her lip, knowing she should've seen this coming. Joseph and Molly had been good enough to look after her all this time. She'd take the gruff tone and the disapproving glances of her uncle anytime over being back with her grandmother.

Wiping the tears from her eyes, she went back downstairs to apologize. When she walked into the kitchen, she saw her aunt alone.

"I'm sorry," Emma blurted to her aunt who had her back turned washing up.

She turned her body around with her

hands still over the sink. "Oh, Emma. I suppose we should've mentioned something before now, but we were waiting to see what would happen. We thought you might find a nice man around these parts."

Emma wrinkled her nose. She'd seen what marriage did to people.

"What's wrong, Emma?"

"Well, I've seen what marriage does. Take Mrs. Esh. Her husband died leaving her with six boys and then she fell ill probably because she was overworked and then she ended up dead." In fact, most of the people Emma had been close to had ended up dead.

"Nonsense. Your *onkel* and I are still alive and we're happy."

"That's true, *jah*." Emma knew that was right because sometimes when she came downstairs to get a drink of water at night she saw them holding hands on the couch. That meant they were happy.

"And everyone dies," her aunt added.

Emma nodded.

"I've written to people I know and we'll see if they know of any suitable men."

"*Jah,* I know. Well, what did you say about me?"

Aunt Molly smiled. "I told them what a lovely girl you are and I told them your age. You'd make a lovely *fraa* for some nice man."

Emma wondered what was really in those letters they'd sent off. "It's my fault really. I should've made some plans before now. I shouldn't have got upset with you and *Onkel* Joseph. You've always been so nice to me and I do appreciate everything, with you taking me in and all."

"You can apologize to him when he comes home. He'll be glad to hear it."

Emma picked up a cloth and helped her aunt clean the kitchen. She hadn't done much thinking about what to do with herself for the future and had hoped things would work themselves out. That was one thing that she had learned from experience—things always found a way to get better even when you least expected it. That was where her cousin, Katie, came in. Over the years she'd been living there, she and her cousin had become best friends and had gotten each other through all kinds of obstacles and difficulties.

Mornings like this were the ones where she wished that her cousin wouldn't sleep in. Her aunt and uncle, although they were kind to her, had one set of rules for Katie and a different set for her. Katie was the only person who could help deflect the situation. It would have been a long shot, but without her, Emma knew she had no chance of getting her uncle and aunt to reconsider their plans.

When Katie woke up, she ran into the kitchen and hugged Emma, with a package in her hands. "Happy birthday." She held out the package to Emma and watched while she unwrapped it.

"*Denke*. Oh, knitted socks."

"They're bed socks. I knitted them myself."

"I never saw you making them."

"I did it at night in my room." Katie giggled.

"*Denke*. My feet get so cold in the winter."

"I know, and so do your hands. They get really chilly."

"You've missed breakfast," Aunt Molly said to Katie in a disapproving tone.

"*Mamm,* you know I have trouble sleeping, and last night I couldn't sleep at all."

"I've told you, you shouldn't have *kaffe* except before midday and not at all after midday. That would keep anybody awake."

Katie pursed her lips. "I don't know if that's true."

"Well, you girls did tell me you are going to do the birthday cake yourselves today."

"*Jah.* We'll have everything organized for dinner, *Mamm,* and you don't have to worry about a thing."

"Emma shouldn't have to cook for her own birthday," Aunt Molly said.

"I like cooking. It'll be fun." Her aunt and uncle never really celebrated birthdays or gave presents. Small gifts would be exchanged at Christmas, but that was all. Katie and Emma always made something to give the other on their birthdays.

"I'm off to visit Irene Lapp. She wasn't feeling too well yesterday and some of the ladies from the knitting circle are visiting to make sure she's all right."

"Okay, we'll see you when you get back, *Mamm,*" Katie said.

CHAPTER 4

*W*hen Aunt Molly had trotted off in her buggy, Emma seized the opportunity to tell Katie what she'd found out.

"You'll never guess what happened today before you woke up. I had a strange conversation with your parents."

Katie screwed up her nose. "I thought I sensed tension in the air as soon as I came downstairs."

"Your *vadder* says it's time I should marry, and he and your *mudder* have already written to some people about me. Asking if they know of a man I could marry." She shook her head. "That's embarrassing, like I can't choose my own man to marry, and not only that, I always thought of marriage as something way off into the future. Then they said I'm supposed to meet some of these men."

"You've just turned twenty. Even I've thought about marriage."

Emma sighed. "I'm different from everyone else, it seems."

"It wouldn't hurt to meet these men. They might be nice."

Emma shook her head. "All they would be would be the leftovers—men who couldn't find their own wives."

"You don't know that for certain. They could be waiting for someone just like you and haven't been able to find someone as good as you."

"Do you think so?"

Katie nodded enthusiastically.

"I don't know."

"Don't worry about it so much, just meet them."

"I suppose so, but I wish they would've asked me about this first."

"You would've said no." Katie laughed.

"I might not have."

"*Jah,* you would've."

Emma laughed. "*Jah,* I guess you're right." If she didn't like any of these men she would have to think about fending for herself. And that would mean finding a job. "I should move out by myself and get a job. That's if I don't like any of these men."

"What would you do?"

"What I've always done. Cook and clean house. I could be a maid. Or, I could help children with their studies." Mrs. Esh had given her a love of learning. Perhaps she could become a teacher? But never having gone to school herself she didn't even know what that would be like.

"You mean you could be a tutor?" Katie asked.

"I guess that's what you'd call it."

"You're very good at reading and you know some history, but if you are thinking of teaching *Englischers,* their teachers have gone to college and you've never even gone to school."

"Well I guess that just leaves cooking and cleaning. There must be a job somewhere. Maybe I could get a live-in job with someone. Where I can live in their house and clean for them too."

"Like a live-in maid?"

"*Jah.* I could do that. That's what I did for Mrs. Esh when I was younger."

"But wouldn't you rather be cleaning your own *haus?*"

"*Jah,* I would, but that's not going to happen anytime soon." She would like that, more than anything. One day she'd have her own place where she could do as she wished.

Everyone she'd lived with had had different rules and different ways of doing things. If she had her own place she could run it the way she wanted.

"What about you, Katie? How long do you think it will be before you marry?" *Or before your parents try to marry you off too?* she thought.

"It depends when I meet the right man. I won't be one of those women who thinks I must get married before I'm twenty, and for sure before twenty-two. I'll marry when I meet someone that I want to spend the rest of my days with."

"Well, that makes sense." Emma hoped that Katie's parents wouldn't force their daughter into a marriage.

Maybe they were trying to find a husband for *her* because they'd had enough of Emma living with them. She probably should've gotten a job before now to contribute to her keep.

"Are you ready to start on the cake?" Katie asked.

"*Jah,* let's do it."

They made a double-layer chocolate cake with plenty of frosting—Emma's favorite part. When Katie's parents arrived home, the two girls had the dinner ready and on the table.

It was during the meal that her aunt and uncle revealed something else to Emma.

"We've had replies from the letters already."

"Really?" Emma looked up at her uncle wondering why he hadn't mentioned that earlier. He was trying to give her little pieces of information—breaking things to her gently, she figured.

"*Jah.*" He put a forkful of chicken into his mouth.

"Can I see the letters?"

"*Nee,*" Aunt Molly said.

Frowning, Emma looked at her aunt wondering where the harm would be.

"Your aunt and I are choosing a couple of men for you to meet. There's no need for you to see the letters. I just wanted you to know that we are taking it seriously and it *is* happening."

"And if I like none of these men?"

Her uncle fixed his eyes on hers and then he waved his fork in the air. "It'll do you no good having that attitude. You've already made up your mind not to like any of them."

Emma gave an impatient huff and wished she could have just one birthday that didn't end up horribly. Looking at the food on her plate, she realized she'd lost her appetite when the crispy chicken skin did nothing to entice her and neither did the creamy mashed potatoes.

If her parents hadn't died in that accident, her life would've been far different. She would've belonged somewhere, been considered precious, and not have been a misfit wherever she went.

"What if I get a job and pay my way? I could pay rent here."

Her aunt looked horrified at that idea. "Emma, we're not doing this for financial reasons. It's for your own good."

"Let's have no more talk of that tonight. I can see it's making you upset, and we want you to be happy on your birthday."

Emma nodded, although it was far too late for that, and pushed her fork into the mashed potatoes. Her uncle had already made his point, that it was happening whether she liked it or not.

CHAPTER 5

When Emma woke a couple of days later, she sat in bed waiting until her uncle left for work. She knew he'd be angry that she didn't come down early for breakfast, but if it wasn't that, he'd find something else to be unhappy about. Since Emma's birthday, she and her uncle had barely spoken. A rift had formed between them. Her aunt and uncle had yet to tell her anything about any of the young men they'd gotten responses from.

The only conclusion Emma could come to was that her would-be husband might be selected for her without her having any say in the matter. It was bad enough that she couldn't just forgo marriage altogether, but what if they tried to take the choice out of her own hands? None of it seemed fair, but as her uncle had reminded her several times recently, life wasn't always fair.

Hearing a knock on her door, she knew it would be her aunt since her cousin never knocked and her uncle never came to her room. "Come in."

Her aunt put her head through the doorway. "Get dressed, Emma. We've got a visitor coming to see you shortly."

"Who is it?"

"A young man." Her aunt gave her what was meant to be a reassuring smile before she closed her door.

Everything weighed heavily on her shoulders as she looked out the window at the gray and gloomy sky. When Emma saw rain droplets on the windowpane, she got off the bed to close her window. It was then she saw a horse and buggy on the road in the distance traveling at quite a speed. She watched as it drew closer, turned off the road and headed onto their long driveway.

The horse trotted up to the front porch, slowing from the gallop that had brought him through the downpour. The man had to have a reckless nature. No one sensible drove a buggy that fast on wet roads. What was so urgent that it couldn't wait for the storm to pass?

Emma didn't like the omen that he'd come in the rain, and how fast he'd driven the horse. That was two strikes against him before she'd even seen his face.

· · ·

THOMAS ESH GALLOPED his horse down the wet streets while the cold wind swept across his face. He loved galloping down lonely streets in the cold. It was times like these that the streets were always deserted. Morgan, his horse and a former racehorse, loved having his head for a good gallop. This was something they both needed. He hadn't taken Morgan out for days, and the horse was definitely feeling his oats. But when Joseph Schwartz's house came into view, it was time to be serious. It was vital to make a good impression.

"Whoa, Morgan. Steady up." With a slight wrist motion on the reins, Morgan slowed. "Right into the next driveway, Morgan. Hopefully, I'll see my future wife unless she has refused me, which I probably wouldn't blame her for if she's found out by now who I am."

Thomas figured talking to his horse was better than talking to himself, which was something he'd grown used to doing in these past years. Hopefully, his lonely days were coming to an end. He hadn't talked to Emma since she was a teenager, back when she was helping out in their household. But he had seen her six months ago at a wedding in her neighboring community. There had been hundreds of guests, and Thomas had made sure that she hadn't seen him. Every time she had turned his way, he made sure he turned in the other direction so only his back was visible.

Something about her had captured his heart that day, and he couldn't believe it when he found that her uncle was trying to find a husband for her. He wrote a very convincing letter to her uncle and then the two men had met a few days ago. Thomas considered that he would be a good provider for her; he was in the process of buying a home close by and then he would join their community. That was something that pleased her uncle that his niece wouldn't have to leave

SAMANTHA PRICE

this community and travel to another to marry.

Thomas had watched her closely at that wedding, and he figured he was a very good judge of people. As a young girl, she'd been quick to laugh, but she'd taken no nonsense from his brothers or, for that matter, from himself.

He could see how she interacted with people at the wedding, that she was a pleasant woman with no nastiness in her. He knew how it affected him that his father had died when he was a young boy, but to lose both parents at a young age, like Emma had, and to be forced to live first with her be-grudging grandmother and then with these relatives was something he couldn't compre-hend. And to have no siblings was another thing he couldn't fathom.

When his mother died, he'd had his brothers to rely on, and now all of them but one was married. A good woman like Emma

46

was just the sort of woman he saw himself with. The only thing was, he wasn't sure what memories she held of him. He'd done many bad things in his past, but he'd confessed them, and they were behind him. But even though those things were in his past, he knew his behavior back then could be the very thing that would stop a woman like Emma from wanting to marry him.

He brought his horse to a walk, driving the buggy from near the porch closer to the cover of the barn, where he secured Morgan. He took off his hat and ran his hand through his hair before putting the hat on his head, and then he lifted the collar of his jacket to keep out the rain. As he walked swiftly to the front door he sent up a silent prayer.

LISTENING CAREFULLY, Emma heard the front door open and close, and then muffled chatter filled the air. It sounded like her uncle was talking to the man, and moments later, she could hear footsteps coming to her room again.

Despite knowing that someone was coming, the knock on Emma's bedroom door startled her.

"Emma, are you ready yet?" her aunt asked.

"Jah, nearly."

"Your *onkel* would like to see you in the living room." Then her voice lowered. "Please make yourself presentable, as well."

What? Wasn't she always presentable? *"Jah,* okay."

"Denke," her aunt said from the other side of the door.

This had to be one of the men they'd told her to expect. Other than that, someone must've died and the man was a messenger. There was no one left she was close to. Unless it was some distant, long lost relative who'd died.

She pulled on her black stockings and then wound her hair on her head, securing it with pins before she placed on her prayer *kapp*. Then she stepped into her shoes, tied them in a double knot and opened her bedroom door.

As she trudged down each step, she told herself again that marriage wasn't for her and she certainly wasn't prepared for it. When she walked into the living room, she saw her uncle sitting by the fireplace and talking to a man who was seated on the couch.

After doing a double take as soon as she saw the man, Emma shook her head in disbelief. It was one of the young men whose mother she'd helped when she was younger, handling the household chores during his mother's lingering illness. She searched the depths of her mind for his name, but it just wouldn't come to her other than that his last name was Esh. He was one of the Esh boys. What was he doing here? Only his face and drunken ways had left memory traces in her mind. He was the son who was a drunkard, a gambler, and—if rumor was correct —worse.

"Oh, there she is," her uncle said, standing up to wave her in. "Thomas, this is my niece, Emma Schwartz."

The man stood up, looked at her and smiled. "It's a pleasure to meet you," he said, the lie apparent in his voice.

Thomas! Hearing the name had jolted her memory; he was indeed the same man she'd thought him to be. She nodded politely, and heat rose in her cheeks when she realized he'd come with the intention of marrying her. He was one of *those* men. Why was he so interested in her when he could have any woman he wanted? And why was he pretending not to know her? She wasn't up for games.

"*Jah,* Thomas Esh and I know each other,

Onkel Joseph. I kept the *haus* for his *mudder* when she was ill some years ago."

Thomas gave a low chuckle and looked embarrassed. *"Jah,* that's true. I didn't know if it was the same young lady so I didn't mention it. I'm sorry about that Joseph."

Joseph frowned at him as though he was trying to work out whether he believed the reason Thomas gave for not mentioning it. He'd looked right at Emma and pretended not to know her. Surely Uncle Joseph had to find that odd.

Thomas was peculiar. He was a good-looking man, but that didn't matter to Emma. She hadn't given him two thoughts since she left the Eshs' house other than when she thought of the Esh boys as a group. He'd been a regular topic of discussion with his mother throughout her days of sickness, though, especially when she knew death was approaching. He was the son she'd worried about the most.

Glancing over at her uncle, Emma let out a long, drawn-out sigh and shook her head in disapproval. Why couldn't Joseph have at least given her some say in the selection process? Thomas was definitely not the man for her and she hoped her uncle had gotten a glimpse of his true nature with that deception that had just taken place. Despite his obvious physical charms he had a dark side, but maybe he wasn't aware that Emma knew that about him.

"Forgive me for my deception, Joseph." After speaking to her uncle he turned to face Emma. "I didn't think you'd remember me, Emma. It was so long ago and you were only a girl back then."

Emma frowned at him, thinking that she'd been seventeen when his mother died, and some Amish girls married at that age. Then she looked open mouthed at her uncle when he seemed, by his silence, to accept Thomas' reason for the deception.

"Emma, I believe Thomas addressed you. Perhaps you should be so kind as to do the same?" Uncle Joseph's voice took on an unpleasant tone.

"Oh, I apologize, *Onkel,*" she said, defiant in her passiveness. "It's good to meet you too, Thomas." She'd play his game back at him and hopefully wiggle out of the game altogether.

Again, Thomas gave an embarrassed laugh while her uncle offered her a grunt of disapproval at her softly veiled sassiness.

She could now hear Katie in the kitchen with her aunt, their voices slightly raised as opposed to normal conversational levels. Had Katie just found out what was going on? Emma was positive that her cousin would take her side, but would that even matter? Her uncle had already chosen whom she'd marry, she was sure of that from the way he'd been talking and he probably even had the plans of the union all ironed out too.

That was the type of businessman Uncle Joseph had always been, so it made sense that such traits, important for making deals with grain, livestock and other farm products, would seep over into the other areas of his life—like making a marriage for his niece.

CHAPTER 6

"So, shall we get down to the heart of the matter?" Thomas asked.

Before she could respond, her uncle answered. "Let's do that, *jah?*" Uncle Joseph pulled out a rolled up piece of paper.

Emma watched in silence, unsure of how to respond. What was that for?

"Excuse me?" she heard her aunt say. When she looked over, her aunt was standing by the kitchen door waving her over. Emma excused herself and stood up. "Come into the kitchen, dear. I believe the men have some business to attend to."

Denke! Emma thought, letting a grin flicker across her face. Things hadn't magically gotten better in a matter of seconds, but her aunt had just saved her from the horror of listening to the specifics of her pre ordained marriage. "Of course, Aunt," she said, hurrying out of the room without a care for what Thomas or her uncle thought of her abrupt exit.

When she walked into the kitchen, however, she was surprised to see the scowling expression that had overtaken Katie's usually happy demeanor.

"*Mamm,* you cannot let *vadder* do this. She turned twenty only recently. Why can't he let her take some time to find a husband?"

"I don't know how to answer that," Aunt Molly said, shaking her head. "You're better at persuading your *vadder* than I am, but I don't think there's any changing his mind on

THE AMISH GIRL WHO NEVER BELONGED (AMIS…

this matter. He's even agreed to pay the dowry if the terms of the agreement are reasonable, so I'd say there's no going back now. I'm sorry, but that's just how it is."

"Dowry? People don't pay dowries anymore, do they?" Katie said. "Anyway, the dowry is usually given to the wife in the form of goods, as far as I'm aware."

Aunt Molly raised her eyebrows. "Your *vadder* is quite willing to pay."

Just then, Katie sighed loudly in disgust, the look on her face speaking volumes for how she felt about the ordeal. "How would he feel if someone was shipping me off to marry some stranger? You and I both know that he wouldn't allow it. Emma is like a *schweschder* to me and a *dochder* to you both. How could he do this, and how can you allow it? Say something to *Dat* and make him stop this nonsense."

"It's for her own good. You'll both understand that when you're older." Aunt Molly turned away, her eyes falling to the floor for some time. When she looked back at the girls, all she said was, "I don't have a say in the matter anyway, but you'll see it's the right thing."

"Don't I have others to meet?" Emma asked hopefully. They had said there'd be others.

Aunt Molly shook her head. Then Emma realized her aunt truly had no say in the matter. Her uncle had most likely met with all of the suitors, and had chosen Thomas without seeing his true nature. Uncle Joseph wouldn't be happy if he knew certain things about Thomas Esh.

Emma knew that it wasn't Aunt Molly's fault at all, but maybe Katie was right. Maybe her mother could at least try to do something to stop it; but her aunt rarely went against her uncle's wishes, so why would this situation be any different?

• • •

THOMAS COULD SEE RIGHT AWAY that things weren't going as planned. It had been a dumb thing to do, to pretend that he didn't know her. She was a woman of great virtue; she didn't appreciate games, and rightly so. He nearly shook his head at himself he was so disappointed. His brother, Phillip, had warned him that he'd get one chance to make a good first impression, and now he'd blown that one chance. He knew Emma was in that kitchen right now giving her aunt one hundred and one reasons why he wasn't the right man for her. His only hope lay in her uncle and keeping him on his side.

"I do apologize, Joseph. I don't know what made me do that."

"I wasn't aware that you knew her."

"I should've told you up front. She helped my *familye* out years ago when my *mudder* was ill. She was *wunderbaar,* caring for all of us at such a young age. She was a good girl who's turned into an incredible woman."

"*Jah,* she's been a great help to Molly and a good example for Katie to look up to, but I need to tell you she can be *againish.*"

Thomas sucked in his lips. He could see for himself that she still had that bullish stubbornness she'd had as a girl. "Sometimes, Joseph, that can be a positive trait."

Joseph slowly smiled. "That's true enough, *jah?*"

Thomas smiled back at him and nodded. "And that is why I would like to make Emma my *fraa,* but, of course, only if she's willing to marry me." He chuckled. "I'm not eager to force someone to marry me. And I'm sure you feel the same."

"She's a sensible girl; she'll see the sense sooner or later. I knew your *vadder* many years ago, and I know you would've come from a good *familye.*"

The first time Thomas had met Joseph, they had discussed that Joseph had known his father. And that was probably the time that he should've told Joseph that he'd already met Emma years before.

Thomas rubbed his chin. "Have I ruined my chances here?"

"*Nay.* I think we should proceed as we discussed and she'll come 'round in time."

"I don't want to put any pressure on her. She seemed distressed about the whole thing. Maybe I should go now, and visit again in a few weeks time when she's calmed down and had time to consider the whole thing?"

"You're here now. It's not necessary to go away and come back again. That will just waste everybody's time."

AS EMMA WAS ABOUT to reassure her aunt that her aunt wasn't to blame, Uncle Joseph walked into the kitchen with Thomas not far behind him. Thomas was grinning as though he'd won some kind of victory.

Thomas looked Emma up and down,

causing Emma to glance down at her dress
and apron. It didn't look too wrinkled or di-
sheveled to her, so why was he staring? Suddenly self-conscious, she smoothed down her
clothes with both hands. She feared he'd be
the kind of man who would tell her how to
dress, what to wear, how to iron, or anything
else that he planned on controlling.

She looked back at Thomas and he was
still grinning at her like a fool.

"*Onkel* Joseph, can you let me know what
exactly is going on? When am I going to be
forced to move from here and marry?" she
asked, as a rush of anger caused her skin to
burn. At this point she didn't care what
anyone thought of her.

Thomas's mouth fell agape as his expression faded to emptiness. There was sadness
in his eyes right then, but despite it, he
leaned toward her and whispered, "You will
be my bride in one month."

Even his voice sounded somber, but

Emma was anything but sympathetic. Instead her body stiffened with anger. More than anything she wanted to avoid her future, but how could she do that now—now that the agreement was made?

Stepping out of the kitchen to avoid speaking her mind, Emma immediately heard footsteps behind her. Turning back, she saw Thomas glaring down at her with his eyebrows pinched together in confusion.

CHAPTER 7

"May I ask where you're going?" Thomas asked.

"Nee!" When she realized how snappy she sounded, she said, "Only if I can ask why you're here," she said, her voice getting louder with every word she spoke. "Why me? Just answer that for me. Of all the women out there to pick from, why would a wealthy man like you possibly choose to marry me and take a dowry from my uncle?" She was well aware the Eshes were wealthy. They probably could've afforded more than one

housekeeper, but for some reason they didn't hire one each time Mrs. Esh fell ill.

Thomas's mouth quickly closed as he shook his head. No answer came, but perhaps that was because her uncle butted in when he came out of the kitchen to join the conversation.

"Emma, will you please be quiet with such nonsense! You must be respectful to Thomas. He has taken the time to come here to offer you a better life, and you batter him with mean-spirited bickering. You should be careful or he could change his mind."

"*Dat!* You cannot do this. I'm done being quiet," Katie said, making her voice heard by her father for the first time since Thomas had stepped foot in the house. "Can't you at least give her some more time?"

"I'm sorry, my girl. I really am, but that doesn't mean I can undo an arrangement. We've agreed and everything is already in motion. You'll both thank me for this one day," he said turning back to Emma.

Enraged and struggling to control her temper, Emma glared at her uncle and said, *"Nee,* we won't—but you might regret this one day. You don't even know Thomas, not really. I could tell you some stories. *Jah,* I could and then you'd be surprised. There were a lot of stories about Thomas back then."

"Emma!" Thomas said almost in a whisper.

"You've not been one to gossip, Emma." Aunt Molly was a little shocked.

"It's not gossip if it's true, is it?" Emma looked at Thomas. "They can probably make me marry you, but they can't make me talk to you or anything else. Good day, Thomas." And with that, Emma turned away and marched up the stairs.

. . .

WHEN KATIE CAME up to her room later, Emma asked, "Is it over? Did he ask Thomas what he'd done?"

Katie shook her head.

Emma opened her mouth in shock. Surely her uncle should've asked him what he'd done and what she'd meant—the stories about him.

Katie slumped next to her on her bed. "How are you feeling?"

Emma shook her head. "Dreadful."

"You really don't like him?"

"Nee."

"What has he done?"

"He was a drinker, a drunkard. I'd find empty bottles of rum behind the barn and I knew it was Thomas who'd left them there in the tall grass. I had to find them and throw them away all the time. And then I heard the brothers talking about how he gambled and lost all his money and then he would go to them asking for more. I heard them lecture him about the gambling and he never denied it. So all of it must have been true. His mother knew it too, and she was worried about him. Mrs. Esh and I talked about everything."

"In between teaching you to read."

"*Jah,* she was a more of a *mudder* to me than my *grossmammi* was, which was sad." Emma sighed thinking about her angry grandmother. "I don't know why my *grossmammi* and I never got along, but we just didn't."

"Maybe you reminded her of the *dochder* she lost."

"*Nee.* She was my *vadder's mudder.*"

"*Ach* sorry. That's right. I wasn't thinking straight."

"And she was some distant relative of yours through your *vadder.* So, anyway, if I reminded her of her son, she should've been nicer to me, *jah?*"

Katie shrugged; she had no answer.

"Anyway, there was worse with Thomas. I heard he got a girl into trouble, a girl who lived in town."

Katie's eyes opened wide. "How did you hear that?"

"I overheard someone saying something at one of the meetings."

"It might've been just gossip. It doesn't mean it was true. You could've overheard gossip."

"I thought that, too, but there must've been something about it that was true otherwise how would the gossip have got started?"

Katie tipped her head to one side. "I don't know, but if it worries you, you should just ask him."

Emma's mouth fell open. "I couldn't possibly speak about something like *that* to him, or any man. It would be too embarrassing."

"Why not? They expect you to marry him, so it's only reasonable that you find out everything about him first, don't you think?"

What Emma thought was that it would just be easier to move on and find somebody else. "And what about him pretending he didn't know me?"

"*Jah,* I know. I overheard that. It was a bit weird."

"And what was I supposed to do—play along with his deceptive games?"

"I guess he thought you'd play along. Otherwise, he wouldn't have done it."

Emma shook her head. "I'm not that kind of person. It just goes to show he doesn't even know me."

"*Nay,* you're not that kind of person. You're kind, honest and lovely. And you need a man just the same as that."

Emma looked at her cousin, glad and grateful that someone was on her side with this whole marrying-her-off business. "I happen to know that Thomas is none of those things."

"That's a shame. He looks so beautiful

and he's so tall and so handsome, and he's got a lovely smile."

Frowning at the sparkle in Katie's eyes, she said, "You marry him then if you like him."

"Not after what you've told me about him."

The two girls giggled, falling backwards onto the bed.

CHAPTER 8

Two nights later, Katie and Emma were whispering in Emma's bedroom. Uncle Joseph was still going ahead with his plans.

"I'll have to leave, Katie, but I don't know where to go."

"Go to Pittsburgh. I think it's the closest city to here and it's only an hour or two away by train."

"That's as good a place as any."

"I had a pen pal from there once a few

years ago. We wrote for a couple of years and then we stopped writing; I'm not sure why."

"That sounds good. And I'm glad it's not too far away. I'll go to Pittsburgh then."

"And what will you do when you get there?"

"The first thing I'll have to do is get a place to stay and find a job as fast as I can."

"I'll give you all the money I've got saved up, nearly eight hundred dollars."

Emma gulped. "You'd do that?"

Emma and Katie had found casual jobs, working at the markets on quite a few Saturdays over the years, and they'd saved all their money.

"Of course I would."

"I'll pay you back as soon as I start working."

"You don't have to pay me back, it's okay."

"I insist. I've got just over five hundred saved. I don't know how long that will keep

me in some kind of a boarding house." Emma
bit her lip.

"If things don't work out, come back."

If Emma didn't find employment she'd
have to come back. She'd put away the
money for her homeward-bound trip, and if
she returned she'd have no choice but to
marry Thomas, or whomever else her uncle
chose. Unless she could quickly find
someone who was nicer than Thomas. "I'm
nervous about this. I never wanted to do this
at all. I wish I had known what your parents
were planning."

"It came as a surprise to me too."

"It reminds me of something my grandmother said." Emma hated thinking about
her grandmother.

After a silent moment, Katie asked,
"What was that?"

"She didn't think girls needed to study or
even know anything apart from cooking and
cleaning. All that there was for a girl, she

said, was motherhood and marriage, and that's why my grandmother didn't even send me to school. It's my fault really. I should've got a permanent job before now rather than doing those smaller jobs. I was living off your parents without a second thought and I can see now that that was wrong of me. Just think, if I had gotten a full-time job two years ago, I could be out living somewhere in my own house right now."

"You would likely be renting a place."

Shaking her head, Emma said, "It wouldn't matter, renting or buying, as long as it was my own place."

"You want to marry eventually, right?"

"Maybe. I guess, I always thought I would one day, but it should just happen naturally. I wonder how my parents met. I don't even know the story. My grandmother never liked to talk about them. I wonder whether they were madly in love? I think they were. They probably met one day and it was love at first sight."

Katie giggled. "Is that how you want things to be with you?"

"*Jah.* I want to look at a man and then he'll look at me and I want sparks to fly, birds to sing and a shaft of light to beam down upon us from *Gott*. He'll know I'm the woman for him and I'll know he's the only man for me.

"Maybe you're expecting too much in a man or expecting him to be someone extra special when really everyone's just…"

"Just what?"

"Everyone's just themselves, no one's extra special. No one's perfect. Everyone has flaws."

"Don't tell me that. I want to believe that the man I'll eventually marry will be someone very special."

"He'll be special to you."

"That's all that matters; he doesn't have to be special to anybody else."

"And how are you to meet this man if you leave the community?"

"I'll figure it out. I'll leave for a few years, just long enough to get some money to come back so I can rent a house of my own and live comfortably. Maybe I'll start some kind of business. I'll be a businesswoman with a string of Amish stores. I'll have an Amish quilt store, sell Amish furniture and every kind of Amish food. I might even open a restaurant."

"*Jah,* you are a good cook."

"*Denke.* And I'll stay away long enough so your parents won't be angry with me when I get back."

Katie giggled. "Like the prodigal son, only you'll be the prodigal cousin three times removed."

"Yeah."

Both girls giggled.

Although Emma was laughing on the outside, inside her stomach was churning away at the thought of having to start over again somewhere else. She didn't like change, and now she was going to have to face another change in her life, the biggest one yet, head on. Not only was she leaving the community, she was leaving everybody she knew and going to a strange town where she knew no one.

She'd have to fully rely on God to make a way for her in this new city.

As soon as Katie went to bed, Emma prayed and poured her heart out to God. She told Him she wouldn't be leaving Him; she'd simply be taking a break from the Amish community. In her heart she'd always be Amish and she promised to hold true to the Amish ways as far as she could, while not living amongst them. She fully intended to come back.

CHAPTER 9

hrough the following day, Emma and her cousin worked together closely in order to plan the one thing that would keep her out of the forced marriage: an escape. It wasn't an easy decision to make, though, especially considering she might not see Katie again for a long time—if ever. With her cousin's full support, she made the difficult choice to seek freedom.

On the third day after Thomas had visited and finalized the arrangement with Uncle

Joseph, Emma made her desperate escape. She took all of the money from her savings and Katie's, which they hoped would be enough to get Emma away and get her on her feet.

"Make sure you write to me whenever you can," Katie said, "but write to me in a different name or *Mamm* and *Dat* will find out where you are. They won't come and get you, but I will get in trouble for writing."

"Are you sure you want to do that? If they find out you've been deceiving them they won't be happy."

"This is something you have to do and you must keep in contact with me. You're the closest thing I have to a *schweschder*."

"I'll write to you under the name of Penny Jones. That's the name of your new pen pal."

"Okay. I'll look forward to your letters, Penny."

Emma knew these were among the last

moments she'd talk to her cousin. At least until Thomas had found another bride. Then, a return, if feasible, could be on the table. There were many possibilities of what the future could bring after such a callous decision like running away, but Emma couldn't focus on them anymore. Only the present mattered, and her freedom.

Katie had helped her pack a small bag; they filled it with *Englisch* clothing they'd purchased at the Goodwill store.

Emma, now dressed in *Englisch* clothing and feeling half-naked with no head covering, paid the taxi driver and got out at the train station ready to step into her future. With her small bag of clothing and other necessities, she hurried toward her train.

The commotion of the station was off-putting, with people walking fast in all directions. Each had a look of determination on their face. It had already been a long morning, so Emma wanted nothing more than to be on her way.

First, she approached the ticket window and bought a ticket.

Emma then followed the signs leading her right up to the train that would take her to Pittsburgh where she could get lost amongst the crowd and find employment.

The first thing she noticed when she got close to the waiting train was lots of people saying goodbye to their loved ones, and others who were greeting *their* loved ones as they were coming off the train. It seemed everyone in the world had family or at least well-wishers but she'd never forgotten her grandmother always calling her a misfit, and that's what she was. Then an announcement was made over the loudspeaker that the train was leaving in one minute.

As she approached the train to climb aboard, a uniformed man stepped in her way and held out his hand.

"Ticket?" he said, his voice sounding rude.

"It's right here," she said, pulling it from her handbag.

The man studied it for what felt like minutes, but then he handed it back and stepped aside with a broad smile. "Enjoy your trip."

Emma thanked him with a smile before stepping up into the train. At first glance, the passenger car wasn't anything spectacular, but the seats were more comfortable than she had expected.

The train was crowded; she was pleased to find a window seat so she could watch the passing scenery. The windows were scratched with all kinds of writing, but she was still able to see through. Without waiting for the trip to start, she laid her head back and closed her eyes, paying attention only to the sounds of the platform and the people around her.

This was the first time she'd been on a

train, and having no one to share the experience with made her fearful rather than excited. Everything was always better when it was shared with someone else.

It was times like these she wished her parents had had another child. If she'd had a sibling they would've been able to face the world together—two peas in a pod. Together they would have suffered through their grandmother's meanness. Yet, with the burden shared it wouldn't have seemed so bad. How helpful it would've been to have a sister or a brother standing next to her at the grave as a seven-year-old child, someone who would've understood how she felt—someone who would've shared her pain.

Out of the corner of her eye, she looked at the man next to her. He was dressed in a suit, probably on his way to work. He was reading a newspaper, and he had a large gold ring and a large gold watch. A man like that would have a family. Opposite Emma was a young woman with headphones; the cord of the headphones ended in her bag which was on her knees, and she too was looking out the window with a glazed-over expression on her face.

Sitting next to the young woman was a man who was texting on his cell phone or, if he wasn't texting, he was doing something that kept making his phone beep every time he touched one of the buttons. It was a little annoying but Emma tried not to let it bother her. What she noticed was that no one looked at anybody else. Even with so many people in one place it was as though everyone was separate.

Emma remembered the talks that the bishop gave. It was a common theme through his talks how the community was a family; although it was made up of many people, it was still one and all of the members were connected to each other.

As she looked around, she saw people

who probably had whole different beliefs from her own. She had to wonder whether she was doing the right thing, walking away from the community like that with no word to the bishop. Running away like this could turn out to be the very worst mistake of her life.

Heading into the unknown was indeed scary. But the alternative was to stay and marry a man of uncertain character. Yes he was Amish, but Amish people were faced with the same temptations and frailties as everybody else. She didn't want to marry a man who was a drunkard—one who might gamble away all the family savings. It was easier to stop something before it started. What if she had married Thomas and had a child with him and then his true colors surfaced? If there was one thing that Emma wanted, it was to provide a safe home for any children she might have. She didn't want any child to go through what she'd gone through and—worst of all—grow up feeling like she, or he, never belonged.

The rest of the ride went by slowly, but Emma was free. Free from the prearranged marriage, and free from the pressure to simply accept such things.

When the train stopped in Pittsburgh, Emma followed the other passengers out of the car. Not knowing what direction to head, she followed the crowd through the station and found herself in the street. Seeing a supermarket, she headed over to buy something to eat.

Just inside the doorway of the supermarket, she spotted a small noticeboard with pieces of paper stuck to it.

As she stepped closer to read the notices, a woman in her thirties or so was sticking a paper to the board. Being immediately struck with curiosity, Emma leaned over to see what she was advertising. It read, "Seeking a trustworthy maid to assist the lady of the house with duties."

"Excuse me," she said, calling out to the woman who had just started walking away.

"Yes?" she said, spinning around with a scrunched brow.

"Are you the one looking for a maid?" she asked, pointing to the paper.

"Oh, well yes, but it's not for me. My sister needs someone. She just lost her previous maid. Are you interested?"

"Actually, yes; yes I am," Emma said, a feeling of hope pulsing in her chest. "I just came here and have no job and no place to stay yet."

"You just got off the train?" The woman looked thoughtful. "Hmm, well I hadn't expected to get an applicant so soon," the woman said, laughing quietly. "My name is Mariah McDonald. If you'd like, you can come back to the house now and meet my sister. She'll interview you. Do you have references?"

"No, but I've had loads of experience."

"Come along then. I'll let her make her own decision."

With that, Emma headed back with Mariah to meet her sister, Mrs. Fields. On the way there, Emma told Mariah that she'd left her Amish community because her uncle was trying to make her marry someone.

That entire first day went from one that was uncertain and scary to one full of hope and good fortune.

She was driven through a neighborhood with large beautiful homes, all of them with pristine gardens where nothing was out of place. And then Mariah pulled into the driveway of a large white two-story home.

"Is this it?" Emma asked peering up at it through the front window of the car.

"Yes, this is my sister's house."

"It's beautiful. I don't think I've ever seen a house this nice."

"Good. Make sure you tell my sister that. She loves compliments."

"I certainly will."

Once out of the car, Emma followed as the woman walked to the front door and rang the bell. A woman of around forty years of age answered the door. Her face was lined and weary. There was a toddler hanging onto her skirt and on one hip she held a baby.

The woman looked from Mariah to Emma.

Mariah said, "I've got someone for you to interview already."

"That was fast."

"I hadn't even put it up on the Internet for you. I had to pick things up from the store near the train station and then I saw a no-ticeboard and I thought why not pop it up there, and that's when I ran into Emma. Emma is an Amish girl."

Mrs. Fields smiled and the tension left her face. It seemed she trusted her immediately once she'd heard she was Amish.

"Um, I'm kind of taking a break now," Emma felt the need to point that out even though she wasn't wearing Amish clothing.

"Nice to meet you, Emma."

"And it's nice to meet you, Mrs. Fields. I must say you have a beautiful home. Are these your children?"

"Yes, this is Ben." She nodded to the baby on her hip. "And this is Jemima," she said of the toddler still clutching her dress.

"Hello, Ben. Hello, Jemima." Emma smiled at the children. "I love children."

"Can you cook, Emma?"

"I can cook, I can clean house, and I can do whatever else you want me to do. Except I can't drive a car."

"Well that's good because that's something I won't need you to do." She looked at her sister. "Can you look after Ben and Jemima while I talk to Emma?"

"Of course I can."

It only took fifteen minutes for Emma to convince Mrs. Fields she was the right woman for the job. She explained that she had just come out of the Amish community because she didn't want to marry the person her uncle had lined up for her.

"Would you be able to live in?" Mrs. Fields asked.

"Yes. I was actually hoping for a live-in job."

"Perfect! When can you start?"

"Right now if you want me to."

"I'll show you to your room. You can start tomorrow; you must be tired after your journey."

"Not really. It wasn't long on the train."

"Where's your luggage?"

"I left it in your sister's car."

Mrs. Fields stood. "I've got a good feeling

about you, Emma. I think we're going to get along just fine."

Emma smiled and stood up as well. "Me too."

Clapping her hands, Mrs. Fields said, "Oh, money."

"Oh, yes. I forgot about money."

Mrs. Fields giggled. "Me too. I'll pay you the standard wage to start with. I don't know what that is, but I will find out. My other lady who just left didn't live here, so her wages would be different than for you."

"That sounds good to me."

"Do you have a bank account?"

"I do."

"Good. I'll let you know what the pay is tonight and then I'll arrange to have it paid into your account every week."

As she followed Mrs. Fields into her new bedroom she paused, closed her eyes and thanked God that this was all working out so perfectly. It seemed God wasn't mad with her for leaving the community, since everything had fallen into place so fast. She never would've dreamed this could happen.

The most pleasant surprise of all was Mrs. Fields's two young children. Emma found them delightful, and they took to her as though they'd always known her.

Emma had a comfortable life with Mrs. Fields. Her bedroom was large and had its own private ensuite. She worked from seven in the morning to seven at night with a three-hour break in the middle of the day. Realistically, the hour she stopped at night was whenever the children were settled in bed. They always had a bit of playtime with Mr. Fields in the evening, before the adults had dinner.

As time ticked on by, things with her new family had only gotten better. Even the thought of returning to Lancaster County had started to become something that she rarely considered anymore. Emma missed her family, though; especially her cousin. She kept her promise to Katie by sending regular letters. Still, her life had gotten better since escaping, and there was no looking back now.

CHAPTER 10

*E*very week Emma got a letter from Katie. She'd found out that her aunt and uncle missed her and Uncle Joseph regretted trying to force her into a marriage. Emma had to wonder if Katie's words were colored with the hope that she would come home, but she didn't belong there now.

Time had a way of going by so fast that you weren't able to stop and realize just how quickly life had changed. Emma had expected things to be different where she was, but she had never imagined that she would

SAMANTHA PRICE

have become part of someone else's family in less than a year. Not only did she serve as the family's only maid, but she also took on duties that maids rarely did. From being a nanny to doing odd jobs, cooking meals and taking the dogs for walks, she did it all and loved every minute of helping Mrs. Fields.

WHILE THE TWO children were having their naps one day, Mrs. Fields had some news.

"I'm going to visit my sister who lives in Lancaster. I believe that's where you're from?"

"Oh, I didn't know you had another sister," Emma said. "And yes, that's where I came from." She knew Mariah lived close by and had never heard Mrs. Fields or Mariah speak of another sister.

"I do. We had a falling out and now she wants to make amends, and she's invited me

100

to her daughter's wedding. It'll take Mariah some time to get back on speaking terms with her, so she won't be going to the wedding with me."

"Oh, that's a shame. Is everyone in your family going?"

"Just me and the two little ones. And I'd like you to come along to help me out."

"I'd love to."

"And maybe you can catch up with some old friends."

Emma nodded. "Oh yes, there's my cousin. I'd really like to see her again."

"Tell me where she lives and I'll arrange to stay close by. As close as we can where there's a reasonable hotel. I do want to stay near some stores, not out in the country somewhere." Mrs. Fields giggled. "Let's get on the Internet now and book something."

"Okay."

Mrs. Fields opened her laptop on the kitchen table and they chose a hotel. It was close to the stores that Emma and Katie used to go to and only blocks from their favorite café.

"There, all booked," Mrs. Fields said when she shut the lid of her laptop.

"I'm so happy to be seeing Katie again."

"I'll make sure you have plenty of time off. The day of the wedding, I'll need you all day. No children are allowed to attend the wedding, so I'll need you to watch them the entire day. The rest of the time is yours."

"Wonderful, thank you. I'll write to Katie right now and tell her I'm coming."

Mrs. Fields smiled. "You and your letters. You're the only person I know who still writes letters."

Emma smiled. She'd told Mrs. Fields she used to be Amish but she couldn't tell her that her letters were written to Katie under an alias. Although she had a suspicion that her employer knew that there were people she wouldn't want to see when she returned.

EMMA STILL FOUND herself longing to see her real family again. She could do without seeing her overbearing uncle if he hadn't gotten over her leaving suddenly, but to see Katie and Aunt Molly once more would make her happy. The reality was that she'd only be able to meet with Katie.

When Emma arrived in Lancaster County, her stomach churned violently. It was either nerves or fear, or most likely a mixture of both.

Mrs. Fields drove her car and it was late in the day when they arrived at the hotel. Emma was immediately shown to her own room and Mrs. Fields gave her a key to the room she shared with her children. Since she was there and being paid she would be required to act as nanny and do any other odd jobs—whatever Mrs. Fields wanted.

The first night they had dinner in the

hotel's restaurant and early the next morning she was given an errand. She was to find Mrs. Fields a simple, sheer stole to cover her shoulders in case the weather turned chilly at the wedding. The wedding was in two days, but the shopping had to be done first thing or Mrs. Fields wouldn't be able to relax. Mrs. Fields took her children to visit her sister for the day and Emma was pleased; that meant she would be able to keep her arrangement with Katie to meet her at their favorite café that afternoon.

She hadn't mentioned to Mrs. Fields that today was her birthday because she didn't want a fuss made. Emma tried to hide the horrible feeling that something was going to go badly wrong. What if Mrs. Fields had brought her back here to terminate her employment, figuring she'd be close to home? She shrugged her concerns away and concentrated on the task ahead.

The busy streets were lined with cars and the occasional Amish buggy.

So much had changed in the past year! She strolled past one of her favorite bakeries only to see that it was now an ice cream parlor. A little further along there was an office building that was in the process of being changed into apartments. With the noise of the traffic behind her, she stood and read the real estate sign outside the soon-to-be luxury apartment building.

A cool breeze rustled through her hair as she turned to make her way down the street. She hoped no Amish people would recognize her since she was in *Englisch* clothing and without the mandatory head covering. Even though she was free of having to wear certain clothing, she still wore a uniform of sorts—a mid-calf-length black skirt and a white blouse, with flat black walking shoes.

The wind picked up and blew a powerful gust, nearly knocking her back a few steps as she walked by the storefronts. She steadied herself and then concentrated on the women's clothing stores she passed to see if they might possibly have a stole that would suit. Sighing, she turned away and crossed a small alleyway to try the next row of stores. As she checked for traffic, she saw an Amish man in the alley, leaning against the wall and smoking.

Then he slowly turned his head to look at Emma. It was Thomas Esh, the very man who'd caused her to leave.

CHAPTER 11

As soon as Thomas saw Emma, he knew he'd done the right thing by befriending Katie and getting her on board with his cause. He'd convinced Katie that he'd always been in love with Emma and she was the only woman for him. Katie wasn't one to stand in the way of love so she risked Emma being cross with her and she had given him the information that Emma's employer was coming there for a wedding. Katie had also given him the name of the hotel in town where they'd be staying.

He couldn't stop staring at Emma. Her light brown hair was free, flowing around her shoulders, and her face still had the inquisitive gaze that suited her so well with her slightly upturned nose.

As their eyes locked onto one another, he immediately regretted that she had seen him smoking. She would add that to her long list of grievances about him. She'd probably heard how he drank too much in his younger days and how he'd been to a poker game and had gambled away all his money and then had to work hard to pay off his debts. She was still looking at him when he threw down the cigarette and crushed it with his foot. Even though he'd planned to 'accidently' run into her, he still wasn't sure what he'd say after all this time had past.

EMMA WAS IMMEDIATELY OVERTAKEN with a range of emotions that she couldn't comprehend. She was aghast and terrified, among many other things. What would he do? She could tell by Thomas' fixed stare that he'd recognized her even in the *Englisch* clothes.

With her chest tightening, Emma shook her head in disbelief, still at a loss for words as he stomped out his cigarette and walked toward her.

Now she felt every bit the runaway that she was. She'd deserted the family who'd taken her in and gone against their wishes and had, no doubt, left them dishonored.

Thomas stood in front of her. She'd been too shocked to move an inch.

"Are you okay, Emma?" His gaze swept over her.

"I'm shocked to see you."

"Why?" he asked as a wry grin creased his lips. "This is where I live. It's you who ran off leaving me feeling like a fool. A man who was set to marry with—"

"What is that supposed to mean?" she asked her voice rising as her skin prickled with anger.

"What are you doing here? Don't you live somewhere else now? I heard you moved far away to escape the dreadful idea of marrying me."

"You do realize that I am free to travel freely and do as I like, *jah?*" she asked, highly annoyed that she'd lapsed into Pennsylvania Dutch. She'd not uttered a word of it since she'd stepped off the platform and onto that train many months ago.

"How did you track me down?" he asked, his hands resting casually on his hips.

That made her laugh. "I didn't track you down."

Thomas stood straighter. "See, now this is exactly why I haven't stopped thinking about you. You have tenacity, and an air about you as though you don't care about impressing anyone. I probably should have just accepted the loss when you ran away, but I couldn't. I'm glad you're back."

She narrowed her eyes at him, annoyed that she found his muscled physique and his height attractive. "I'm not back. I'm visiting and I'm not in the community anymore if you hadn't noticed."

"I don't exactly know what to say to that," he said still staring at her with large dark eyes.

"There's nothing that you need to say."

"What are you doing here in town? Have you changed your mind and now you've come back to me?"

She ignored that last question. "I'm shopping for my employer."

He raised his eyebrows. "Maybe I can help. We can talk on the way. I'd like to know what you've been doing. And I know the stores well and I can help you find things."

Shaking her head, she said, "I know the stores. This is where Katie and I used to shop."

"Some things have changed."

She shrugged her shoulders. "I don't want you to utter even one word about marriage or me running away."

"Okay."

Emma was hesitant, still apprehensive of his true intentions. "And I don't want you to mention to my *onkel* you've seen me."

"Done. I can do most of the talking. After all, I'm the one with all the explaining and apologizing to do," he said, staring deep into her eyes.

Well, that was a turnabout. "You know you have apologizing to do to me?"

"*Jah.* Things didn't work out for us, and thinking back, you would've felt like all choice had been taken out of your hands. For that, I'm sorry."

Slowly, she nodded. "Well, that means a lot. It really does. *Denke.*"

Now grinning, he stepped forward. "Shall we go shopping?"

With his bright smile and soft eyes, it was difficult for Emma not to trust him enough to just talk. It didn't hurt that he was handsome, but all that aside, she wanted to know his opinion of how her family was. "Do you happen to know which store would sell a sheer cape?" she asked.

"A cape? Like for an action hero?"

Emma laughed. "*Nee.* A lady's cape—a stole. Something a lady puts around her shoulders on a cold night."

"You've got me on that one. But I can show you to some dress shops that might have something like that."

Emma sighed. "I don't know that you'll be much help to me."

"That's starting to be a reoccurring pattern. Let me try to make things up to you."

"Okay. I guess that wouldn't hurt." She could tell he liked her and, for the first time, she felt a little attraction to him and it hadn't anything to do with his looks. He had a quick mind and he was intelligent. And he'd apologized to her without prompting. If only he didn't have all those bad habits.

CHAPTER 12

*A*s they moved further from the alleyway, Emma found herself buried under the weight of uncertainty. She'd agreed he could come with her and she wasn't certain why. If someone happened to see him, they'd take a better look at her to see why he was with an *Englischer.* She thought it could turn out badly for both of them.

Emma stopped still. "Um, I don't think this is a good idea."

"What?" He stopped too, and turned to face her.

"Being seen with you."

His dark eyebrows drew together. "I won't tell your *onkel*."

This time it wasn't her uncle she was worried about. "Someone else might see us together."

"Is that all?" he asked.

Emma nodded, remembering how she hadn't even told the bishop she was leaving. What if word got back to him that she'd been in town and hadn't even gotten in touch with anyone except for cousin Katie, and Thomas, the man she'd rejected? That would look bad for her, and especially bad for Thomas.

"Wait here a minute." He dashed back into the alley and when he returned, he had no hat and he'd taken off his suspenders. His white shirt billowed out and was not tucked into his black trousers.

Emma couldn't help laughing when he

walked back toward her. "Is that your idea of a disguise?"

"*Jah.*" He looked down at himself with his arms well away from his sides. "It's the best I can do, under the circumstances. Do you like it?"

"I suppose you won't stand out so much."

After walking through the busy streets, they turned onto a quiet road with a small store at its far end. Emma was a bit confused why a dress shop would be so isolated from the rest of the businesses, but a large white sign made her focus on that instead. 'Chez Lynne,' it read, and before they even reached the door, a short, older woman greeted them with a pleasant smile.

"Good morning!" the woman called out, sounding excited. "Or is it afternoon? I can't even remember anymore," she added, laughing as she held the door open for them.

They walked into the store, which Emma

could now see was more of a business that sold fabrics. Beautiful fabrics.

"Hello again," Thomas said, as if he already knew the woman. "When I was here to get the materials for my suits, you mentioned having the finest fabrics for women."

"I sure do," the woman said, not missing a beat. Without saying anything else, she knelt down behind the counter and re-emerged with several samples in her hands. "These are the best we have."

Emma smiled, realizing just how lovely the soft silk materials were. "I haven't seen this kind of quality in months," she said, rubbing one of the samples with her fingers. "I'm after a sheer stole. I'm shopping for someone else and she would like a plain stole of sheer fabric. Maybe a silver or a cream color?"

"Yes, we have those. At least we had some. I'll go see what we've got." The woman went to the back of the store and came back with two options. The first had a subtle tone-on-tone pattern of cream roses, but at first look it was plain and all silky cream. The second was a sheer white stole.

"I think the cream one will do nicely. I'll take it."

"Good. I'll wrap it for you."

As the kind old woman packaged her purchase, Emma couldn't help but be thankful for Thomas. He'd just saved her from having to deal with a disappointed employer. Because of all the good, she was slowly beginning to worry that bad would soon follow. Wasn't that how it always happened?

When the shopkeeper read the total aloud, Emma dug through her handbag for the money. By the time she looked up, however, Thomas had already paid in her stead. "What are you doing?" she asked, shaking her head in disbelief.

"Excuse me? Oh, well, consider this part of my apology," he said, handing her the small bag. "Come, and I'll give you the other part next."

Curious but worried, Emma thanked the woman before following Thomas back out of the store. He'd walked on ahead, so she had to run a bit to catch up, intent on knowing what his deal really was. "Stop!" she said, shouting. "Please, just tell me what this is all about."

"All right then," he said, walking back toward her.

There, in the middle of a quiet street just off the main stretch of businesses, the two stood eye-to-eye.

"*Gott* led you to me today because I asked Him if He might bring you back to me. And I will be honest with you for the first time. Since the days when you worked for my *mudder,* I'd always liked you as a person. You were kind and good. Years later, well after I'd lost track of what had become of you, I heard rumors your *onkel* was looking to find you a husband. I took that chance. I really did mess it up though, didn't I? I should've befriended you and let things happen naturally, but I felt like time was against me." He shook his head. "That clumsy proposal was awful and your *onkel* was so keen to force things... I am so sorry for my actions. I know it put you under so much pressure that you had no choice but to run away." He lowered his eyes.

Emma's chest tightened as the words found their way to her heart, but it was still tough to digest. How was she to know if that was the truth or not? He'd said he was being honest, but what if it was just a new set of lies to win her over with? Going behind her back and dealing with her uncle was almost unforgivable, but it was the gossip she'd heard about him that gave her the biggest reason to question him. Was he still a secretive drunkard with no morals and a cold heart?

CHAPTER 13

With apprehension gripping her, Emma glanced back up at Thomas to see his eyes again. Now, they were even glossier, with a red swell around them. If she hadn't known any better, she would have guessed that he was close to tears. It was strange though, because she now saw softness in him, a kindness that had always been hidden by an overbearing and too-confident personality. Had she been completely wrong about him?

"Well, I don't really know what to say. You've left me speechless far too many times for one day!" Emma laughed nervously.

Thomas smiled, his cheeks reddening at her comment. "I apologize for that as well," he said. "Why don't we start with that friendship? What do you say?"

Emma smiled, humbled by how he was acting toward her. It felt like he truly meant every word that had come out of his mouth. "Well, I think that would be lovely on one condition. I have to insist we be discreet. I took on another name in my letters to Katie so my *onkel* wouldn't know they came from me. I ask that you keep those letters to Katie between us. I don't want to get her into trouble."

Thomas grinned from ear to ear. "You're not so different from me. That is the easiest condition I've had to meet for an agreement in a long time. Of course I'll keep that between us. Your secret is safe with me."

"Good. Well, it was nice seeing you again." She surprised herself that she really meant it.

"Maybe we can meet for lunch or something in the next few days? How about tomorrow?" Thomas asked.

"I thank you for helping me, but—"

"I'll keep your secret even if you don't meet me for lunch."

"Oh, well. The lady I work for might not give me the time off. I usually have to look after the two young children."

His mouth turned down at the corners. He pointed to a café. "See that place there? I'll be waiting for you there tomorrow at one o'clock in the hopes that you'll join me. And I'm sorry from the bottom of my heart for the foolishness that drove you away." He shook his head. "I never wanted that to happen."

She was pleased he was man enough to actually say he was sorry, and she was starting to believe he meant it. "I'll try to meet you," she said, even though she knew already that Mrs. Fields would give her the time off if she asked for it. Mrs. Fields had already said she only needed her to watch the children on the day of the wedding. Then she couldn't resist reaching up and touching his chocolate brown hair. "You better go and find your hat."

His face broke into a smile. "I hope I see you tomorrow."

"I will try," she said walking away from him. She headed three blocks away where she'd arranged to meet Katie.

Katie was waiting outside the café they used to go to. She ran to her and they hugged each other. Then they went inside, hoping they wouldn't be seen together so word wouldn't get back to Uncle Joseph.

"It's so good to see you. What's the hotel like?"

Katie hadn't changed one little bit. She still had her bright hazel eyes and the same freckles that dotted her cheeks and ran across her nose.

"It's lovely. I have an extra bed and the children will probably stay in my room overnight when Mrs. Fields goes to the wedding. Katie, it's the strangest thing. I just saw Thomas."

"Thomas Esh?"

"Yes. What's going on with him?" There was a light inside Emma. Maybe Thomas wasn't as bad as she'd always thought.

"He's moved *haus* and now he goes to our meetings. He's in our very community."

"Oh. You didn't tell me that, and he didn't mention it either."

"Well, we don't talk about him in our letters," Katie was quick to point out.

"I guess that's true. I think I might have misjudged him. He seemed lovely just now and even came with me to a store when I had to buy something for Mrs. Fields."

"I haven't had much to do with him. He doesn't hang around with my crowd because he's older."

"Do you think he's a good person?"

"*Jah,* I think so. I've heard nothing to make me think he isn't." A smile spread across Katie's face. "You like him, don't you? I can tell."

"No. Well, maybe a little bit." Emma giggled.

"What did he say?"

"He wants to get to know me and start off as friends. He's asked me for lunch tomorrow."

Katie gasped and her eyes grew wide. "Are you going?"

"I think I might. Mrs. Fields said I could take time off while I'm here except for the day of the wedding."

"Well, you must meet me after you've seen him and tell me everything."

"I'm meeting him at one, so how about I meet you at three? Then I can be back to the hotel in time to help feed and bathe the children."

"Okay."

CHAPTER 14

The next day, Emma awoke to the sound of birds chirping outside her window. Sitting up, she leaned over and glanced out over the town. The hotel was right in the midst of a busy street, but the birds didn't seem to mind the noise below in the least. She wondered how they could seem so cheerful so early in the morning.

At eight, as arranged, she met Mrs. Fields and the children for breakfast in the hotel dining room. As soon as she sat down she greeted them all and then asked, "Mrs. Fields, would you mind if I met a friend for lunch at one today?"

"I'd be delighted to see you take time off and have some time to yourself. Take the day off. I told you I only need you tomorrow, the day of the wedding."

"The whole day?"

"You rarely have time off. Even on your days off you're still helping me. No, you go and enjoy yourself. Would this friend of yours be a male?"

Emma felt her cheeks heat and hoped she wasn't going red. "He is."

"And this man is around your age?"

Emma giggled. "He's an old friend. And he's quite a few years older."

"Sometimes an older man is better. Neil is ten years older than I am."

"Oh, I didn't realize that, but I knew he was older." Emma glanced at the children. "I hope they won't be too much for you today."

"No. I'll visit my sister again and they can play with her children. They're older, but they love children."

"That sounds like they'll have fun," Emma said, wiping some food off Jemima's chin.

Mrs. Fields took the napkin out of Emma's hands. "Your time off starts from now. Think about yourself for a change."

Emma smiled and nodded. "I appreciate that."

Lunch plans had already been made, but Emma wondered if Thomas was having second thoughts now. She hoped Thomas would be there because when they'd spoken yesterday, she hadn't given him much hope that she'd show up.

Emma excused herself as soon as breakfast was over, and headed to her room. At lunch she'd find out more about Thomas' character and she'd ask him a few hard questions. With that in mind, she became determined to look her very best that day. Over the next hour or so, she washed up, pressed her dress carefully, and even put on a scant amount of makeup. Her dress was pale blue and sleeveless, and modestly cut, reaching nearly to her knees. On her feet were strappy white sandals with a small heel.

In reality, the walk to the café didn't take too long, but in Emma's mind, time slowed to a crawl. Every step filled her with apprehension and trepidation, as her lunch date with Thomas got closer. There was a pit in her stomach that seemed to grow larger and larger, and it churned more violently with each passing moment.

When she found the café again, Emma walked up to the front door. She was a little earlier than scheduled to give her nerves a chance to settle, and perhaps Thomas would be there soon enough if he hadn't changed his mind.

When Emma entered, a young woman with a friendly smile met her. "Good afternoon, may I get you seated?"

"Yes, please," she replied, looking around the dining area. "I was supposed to meet a friend here, but I think I'm a bit early—" In the middle of her sentence, she paused abruptly, realizing that Thomas was already there. He was sitting off at a small table all by himself; only one other chair was at the table.

"Oh, you must be here for Thomas. Come through," the woman said, as she tucked her long blonde hair behind her ear and led her to the table.

Thomas jumped to his feet when he saw her approach. When they both took their seats, Emma realized he hadn't taken his eyes off her. She wondered what he was thinking. Something made her want to know him more. There was a warm familiarity about him. Probably because he reminded her of the time she had spent with his family and his lovely mother.

"I'm so happy you came." He flashed his handsome smile.

"Um, my employer gave me the time off."

"I didn't expect you to arrive just minutes after I did, but I'm glad you're here. Maybe that means we are both just as excited to see the other," Thomas said. "Anyway, your employer is very fortunate. I remember what a hard worker you were. My brothers and I felt sorry for you."

"I recall you all helped when you came home."

"Hmm. Probably not enough."

"It was. You couldn't have done more with all your hard work on the farm. I've heard what hard work a dairy farm is." Emma was still trying to calm her heart from beating so fast, but there were so many emotions at play that she couldn't control how she felt. His handsome face couldn't be allowed to distract her. What was inside was more important, she reminded herself and that was what she had to find out.

"Is something wrong?" he asked frowning. "You seem a bit ... worried or upset."

"Oh, no, not at all," Emma said. "Well," she sighed, realizing that the truth might be her only saving grace. "I guess I'm just a bit worried about something. I didn't give you a chance when you came to the house that day."

"No one let *you* have a chance that day. You were forced into things, and your only choice was to run."

"Many years ago, back when I stayed with your family, there were rumors about you and those rumors weren't good."

His gaze left her eyes and fell to the table. "I'm not proud of myself and what I used to do. I no longer gamble and I've given up drinking. I haven't had one drop for two years."

"Oh, that is good."

"I have a cigarette every now and again."

Emma nodded. "I realized I didn't give you a chance before I ran away. But, the choice of a husband is mine to make and I don't want anyone making that choice for me no matter how well intentioned that person might be."

"Your *onkel?*"

"*Jah,* my *onkel.*"

The waitress asked what they'd like to order. They hadn't even had a chance to look in the menus.

"I come here a lot. The hamburgers are good," he said to Emma.

"I'll have one then," Emma said.

"Two with the works, thanks."

"Sure, Thomas." The waitress gave him a

special smile before she walked away, but he didn't seem to notice and set his eyes back onto Emma.

"Let's get reacquainted. I hope you don't have a boyfriend."

CHAPTER 15

*E*mma smiled at him. "If I did have one, I wouldn't be here with you."

"That's a relief," he said, holding his heart dramatically. That made Emma giggle.

"What about you?" Emma asked.

Thomas shook his head. "I don't have a boyfriend either."

Emma giggled again. "A girlfriend, I meant."

"I don't." He sighed. "A woman broke my heart a year ago and I'm hoping to find someone to repair the gaping hole she left."

A year ago was when she ran away. "You mean me?"

He nodded.

Emma cleared her throat and straightened up. She didn't want a man who was good at sweet talking, she wanted honesty, and for all she knew he could be lying about everything he'd just said. What if he hadn't really changed at all?

"There it is, that troubled look again."

"Thomas, how do I know you're telling me the truth about everything you're saying?"

He drew his dark eyebrows together. "I never thought for a moment you wouldn't believe me. I have changed, Emma. The change started when my mother died." They were both silent a moment. "My mother said something to me before she died, just days before she died."

"What did she say?"

"She said that I should marry someone

like you, a woman with a good heart. Back then you were just a girl in your teens, and I was only interested in women much older, closer to my age. When I heard your *onkel* was looking for a husband for you, I was looking for a *fraa,* and my *mudder's* words came back to me."

"Oh."

"I didn't know you'd think so poorly of me."

Emma huffed a sigh. "Well, when you said hello to me in front of *Onkel* Joseph you pretended not to know me. I didn't think you'd do that if your intentions were sincere."

"I've always been a fool and a prankster. I honestly don't know what made me do that. Maybe it was nerves, not knowing how you'd take to finding out I had contacted your *onkel*. I wasn't sure if he had your consent, or how you felt about the whole thing."

"That's just it. He didn't have my consent."

"I figured that out pretty quickly when I got there. I'm sorry for the deception."

She nodded. If he confessed and was honest, she could forgive him. "I'm pleased Mrs. Esh thought so highly of me."

"She did. You were like a *dochder* to her. I'm sure she would've preferred to have some girls instead of a family of all boys."

"When did your *vadder* die? I was always too scared to ask your *mudder*. I didn't want to make her sad. She was always so frail."

"He died when I was ten. On my tenth birthday."

"*Ach nee.* That's awful."

"*Jah,* since then I've always had bad things happen on my birthday."

Emma nodded. "Me too."

"I found out that my *mudder* had cancer on my eleventh birthday."

"I'm sorry. That's so sad."

Thomas' looked so upset that Emma decided to share a story of her own. "My parents' funeral was held on my seventh birthday. It was awful and I have a dread of birthdays now." She looked up at him under her lashes. "It was my birthday when my uncle told me he was looking for a man for me to marry and you came to the house about two days later."

A look of delight crossed his face. "Yesterday was your birthday?"

"How did you know that?"

"When I came to your house it had been *my* birthday two days before."

"Is your birthday the fifth of September?"

He chuckled. *"Jah.* We share the same birthday."

Emma giggled. "And the same fear of that day, it seems."

He nodded. *"Jah.* My *mudder* never celebrated birthdays. No mention was made of them from the time my *vadder* died."

"We would've realized we'd shared that day if ... if there was some celebration to be had back then. I would have been there at your house for at least two or three of those birthdays over the two stays I was there. And your mother's death was close to our birthday, too, because I turned seventeen then."

"I think she stopped celebrating birthdays for my sake. If a fuss was made, I think she thought I'd remember what happened to my *vadder* more. It would make it seem somehow worse, if that's possible."

"And you'd have been jealous of your brothers because they would've been happy when they celebrated their birthdays. Hmm. She was a wise woman."

"I don't know that I'd have been jealous of my brothers."

Emma shook her head. "Yes you would. All you boys were competitive."

She saw a gleam in his eyes when he said,

146

"Brothers are always like that. That's the way boys are. We weren't jealous in a bad way."

"There's a good way to be jealous?"

He scratched his chin slowly. "I can see I have to be careful what I say around you."

The waitress brought their burgers and quickly left after she had placed them on the table.

"Oh, this is huge." Emma looked at it, wondering how to go about eating it. No wonder there were knives and forks on the table. It wasn't a burger she could pick up and eat with her hands.

"Wait until you try it. These are the best hamburgers for miles."

After she had picked up knife and fork, she said, "I can't wait to try it. It looks good."

"What if we start again, Emma, with no pressure? We've found out we've got a few things in common, and I'm not the bad person you thought I was. Well, I was, but I've evolved."

Emma stared back but said nothing. She was completely speechless, caught off guard even still by just how nice he seemed. There was so much more to Thomas than she had ever known.

He chuckled. "Say something, Emma. Don't leave me wondering."

"I'd like to get to know you better, but we leave in a couple of days. I'm not even sure when."

"Then stay here. I'll arrange for you to stay with a nice *familye,* if you don't want to stay back at Joseph's *haus.*"

Emma sighed. "I couldn't just quit my job. We could write to each other."

He shook his head. "That's not how I imagined this going. I'd love it if you'd take a chance and marry me. Marry me right now —today."

Emma giggled. "I can't. I barely know you."

"You know me well enough. I'm a good man, and I'll look after you. With the money *Mamm* left me, I invested it for a few years and recently I bought a small *haus*. I've built onto it so it has an upper level that overlooks a river. You'll love it. I'm sure you will."

"It sounds nice. You didn't tell me you'd moved and you're in my old community now."

"I thought you might have known. You said you keep in touch with Katie, didn't she tell you?"

"She did, actually."

"I see. I've got a good job working… well, I've really got two jobs."

"You're not working today."

"I took time off to see you again," he said.

"What are your jobs?" Maybe he had turned his life around. A gambling drunkard wouldn't be able to keep two jobs for long.

"I'm a building foreman and when I'm not doing that, I make furniture in my barn at home and sell it in my *bruder's* store."

"Which *bruder*?"

"David. His store is doing so well, he's got plans for a second one."

"David ... he was the youngest, wasn't he?"

"That's right and he's done the best for himself."

"Perhaps I should marry him?"

Thomas laughed. "Well, you could've but that position has already been taken, six months ago, by a lovely young lady named Amy." He took another bite of his hamburger.

CHAPTER 16

While Emma thought about what he had said, she cut a piece of meat with fork and knife and popped it into her mouth. Being with him was pleasant but that wasn't enough; she wasn't going to rush into a marriage and risk regretting it. It seemed smarter to wait even if another girl took his attention in the meantime, if he grew impatient. When she had swallowed, she said, "We'll have to write."

"Okay. We'll write if that's the way to

your heart."

"I didn't say it was, but that's the only way we can keep in contact. If you still want to."

"When do you leave?"

"I'm not certain. I think Mrs. Fields wants to stay a couple more days after the wedding to spend time with her sister and then we leave."

"Do you have a cell phone?"

"Yes, Mrs. Fields gave me one so she could contact me when she's out."

"Great. I'll get your number and we can talk on the phone. I've got a phone in my barn."

Emma nodded. "Okay."

"Oh, one thing I didn't ask. One very important thing."

"What's that?"

"If things go well between us and you fall madly and hopelessly in love with me, would you come back to the community?"

"I would. I'd like that very much. I don't belong in the *Englisch* world. I go to church with the Fields family every Sunday. It's good, but it's not the same."

"Ah, so you only left because you were running away from marriage, but more importantly, away from me?"

She picked up the paper napkin and dabbed at the corners of her mouth. "That's about right. I never wanted to leave the community, but I felt I had no choice. I thought you knew that. If I had gone to a different community, word would've gotten around where I was. Just as word got around that my *onkel* was looking for a husband for me."

He nodded and she hoped he appreciated her being as honest as she could possibly be.

"I'm meeting Katie this afternoon," she said.

"That'll be nice?"

"Yes. I nearly didn't call her because I don't like her having to keep secret that I'm in town, but she's the only family I have, she and her parents."

"Why don't you go back and live with them?"

Emma laughed. "I can't. I'm too old. Old enough I ought not to be a burden on them."

"Well, you could get a job around here. I'll ask David. I'm sure he'd find you a job in his store, or even the new one when it's up and running."

"That's kind, but I must go back with Mrs. Fields."

He breathed out heavily and stared at her. "I hate it when I don't get my own way."

"Anyway, if I moved back with Katie, it would make things awkward. I'm still not sure of my *onkel's* motivations in trying to have me marry you."

"He only has your best interests in mind."

"I guess. But it seems to me that I ought

to have some input into what my best interests are."

"I understand that. I'd be able to visit you once or twice a week if you lived with them, and that's better than you being two hours away."

"Let me think about it."

He leaned forward. "Will you really?"

"Yes."

He smiled. "I would've loved to show you my *haus* today. What are you doing tomorrow?"

"I can't see you tomorrow. I have the two young children all day because Mrs. Fields will be at her niece's wedding."

"Perfect. Bring them too. I bet they'd love to go on a buggy ride and have ice-cream."

Emma giggled. "Really? Doesn't that mean you'll have to take another day off?"

"I haven't had a vacation in years, so I'm sure I can have a day off every now and again. What do you say?"

"Okay. As long as it's all right with their mother."

"I'll call you tonight and find out. Where are you staying?"

Emma gave him the name of the hotel and her room number.

"Make sure you answer the phone."

"I will."

"I'll call at eight."

"Okay. The children go to bed at seven thirty, so I'll be back in my room by then."

"Good. I hope she says they can go."

Emma liked the attention he was giving her. His marriage proposal was given in a joking manner, but he seemed genuinely delighted to see her again. Other young men had driven her home after singings before but that was never anything serious. Since she'd left the Amish, she hadn't even been on one date. It was hard to meet people when she mostly stayed home all the time and looked after the children.

156

Emma left Thomas just in time to meet Katie at a different café. It seemed all of her free time there had been spent in cafés.

When she walked in she saw Katie sitting at a table by the window.

She rushed over and sat down with her.

"How did your lunch go?" Katie asked.

"Everything happened so quickly it was like a whirlwind. He talks at a million miles an hour and…" she shook her head. "He's lovely to look at. Not that his handsome face is influencing me. I know that the inner part of a man is the important part."

"You've got that right. Now tell me exactly what happened right from the start."

Emma told Katie everything that she could remember.

"He proposed?"

"He was joking, I'm sure."

"You look pretty happy."

Emma nodded. She felt happy.

"And he's taking you and the children in the buggy tomorrow?"

"As long as it's all right with Mrs. Fields. He wants to show me his *haus*." Emma leaned across the table. "He told me he's moved to your community. You must've seen something of him. What do you truly think of him?"

"He really really likes you."

Emma laughed. "I got that impression, but what do *you* think? You know the stories I've heard of him. He tells me he's changed, but it makes me hesitant. What you think about him means a lot to me." Emma stared at her cousin waiting for her to respond.

"I like him and if you want to know what I think, I think he'd be perfect for you. Girls have liked him and he's chosen no one. It's as though he's waiting for you. Now what shall we eat?"

"I'll just have to sit here and watch you. I couldn't possibly eat or drink another thing."

CHAPTER 17

hen Mrs. Fields arrived back
at the hotel, Emma was
waiting for her.

"How was your day?" Emma asked her.

"We had a lovely time, but I'm a little
worn out."

Emma looked down at the children and
saw that their clothes and faces were a little
grubby. "It looks like Ben and Jemima had a
good time, too."

"They played in the sandpit most of the
day with their cousins. They've still got all

their play equipment in the backyard from when they were younger."

"I'll give them a bath."

"Thank you, Emma. I'd appreciate that. Could I use your bathroom to have a shower and then I'll meet you downstairs for dinner?"

"Sure."

"I'll go down first because I need to sit down with a drink. My sister doesn't drink, and you know how I like a glass every evening."

Mrs. Fields's bathroom had a bathtub, whereas Emma's bathroom only had a shower.

Remembering that Thomas had said he'd call her room at eight, she said, "Why don't the children and I meet you downstairs at six thirty?" By downstairs Emma meant the restaurant on the first floor of the hotel.

"Perfect. I'll see you then."

While bathing the children, she was thinking of ways to ask Mrs. Fields about taking the children out with Thomas for the day. She was almost sure their mother wouldn't mind, but if she said 'no' that would mean that she wouldn't see Thomas again before she left. For the first time, Emma found herself wanting to see Thomas, even looking forward to it.

She'd certainly misjudged him without getting to know him again after the years that had passed since she'd helped his mother. But she wasn't going to be quick to let her heart overrule her head. Tomorrow she hoped she'd find out more about his character and his personality. With Ben and Jemima there she would also see how he interacted with children. She'd never seen Thomas around children.

It seemed strange that he was the only one of his brothers to remain unmarried. He certainly had the looks and the personality.

Perhaps there was something wrong with him. Only time would tell.

Once she'd dried off eighteen-month-old Ben and two-and-a-half year old Jemima, she changed them into some clean clothes.

"Okay, you both set for dinner?" she asked them.

Ben stared her through big round blue eyes while Jemima said, "Yes, I hungy and tirsty."

"Oh, you're hungry and thirsty?"

Jemima nodded, and Ben copied his sister with a nod of his own.

"We'll have to do something about that. Let's go downstairs and find your mother so we can all have dinner together."

"Mummy," Ben said.

"Yes, we'll go down and find your mummy at the restaurant."

Jemima jumped up and down, and Emma hoisted Ben onto her hip and held Jemima's hand as she headed out of the hotel room.

· · ·

EMMA WAVED to Mrs. Fields when she saw her at the bar, and soon they were all seated at a table in the large restaurant. The children were always well behaved when they were out, and they were good eaters. Ben was in a highchair and Jemima sat in a chair fitted with a booster seat. The children were between the two women.

"I didn't even ask how your day was, Emma," Mrs. Fields said after they had ordered their meal.

Emma cleared her throat. "I had lunch with an old friend, and he wants to know if the children and I can go and see his house tomorrow. That would mean riding in a buggy, if that's all right with you."

"As long as the children are with you, I know they'll be safe. I have every confidence in you."

Emma smiled; that was exactly what she

had hoped Mrs. Fields would say. "Thank you. I'll know they'll have such fun. They'll be able to see animals and horses too."

"More importantly, is this man the reason you've been so happy lately?"

"Oh, I didn't know I'd been any different."

"You've got a light about your face and your eyes, and that wasn't there before."

"That's interesting."

"Tell me about him."

Ben started banging on the tray of his highchair. Emma reached into her bag and pulled out two toys to keep the children occupied. "It's quite a long story and it goes back many years."

"I love a good story."

Emma told her the story of how she'd first met Thomas, the stories she'd heard about him and that he was the reason that she left Lancaster.

"It's probably all my fault." Mrs. Fields had a twinkle in her eye.

"What is your fault?" Emma asked.

Mrs. Fields said, "I prayed that you would meet a nice man, but while I was praying I thought you would meet someone from my church. Now here we are in Lancaster."

"You prayed for me? How thoughtful."

"I always pray for you and count you amongst the prayers every time I pray for my family."

"Thank you. That means a lot to me."

Then their meals were served, which interrupted their flow of conversation. Emma cut up the children's food. Ben and Jemima were having fish and chips, something that they could feed themselves and Emma cut their fish into tiny pieces, making sure there were no bones.

CHAPTER 18

*A*fter Emma had said good night to Mrs. Fields and the two children, she hurried back to her room to wait for Thomas's call. She looked at the digital clock on the bedside table. It read seven fifty. What if he never called at all? She'd look like a fool in front of Mrs. Fields since she had told her all about Thomas and Mrs. Fields had given her permission for the children to visit his farm. Mrs. Fields was excited for her, too.

Emma got ready for bed and brushed out

her long hair. Not long after she'd left the community she'd cut her hair to halfway down her back. Before that, it was almost to her knees since she'd never had it cut. It was still long by other people's standards. As she pulled the brush through her hair, the phone rang. Her heart pumped hard against her chest and she let it ring twice so she wouldn't seem as though she'd been sitting over the phone waiting for his call.

She picked it up on the third ring. "Hello."

"Hello, Emma. What's the news?"

Emma was both relieved and pleased to hear his deep voice. "We're allowed to go."

"That is good news. Why don't I collect you from the hotel at around eight o'clock and then we can have a full day together?"

"Are you sure you can spare the time?"

"Trust me; I've got everything arranged."

Emma heard a soft chuckle escape his lips. She was excited at the idea of learning more about him and the person he'd become. "We'll be waiting out front at eight o'clock. I'll try to be on time unless I have to change Ben's diaper at the last minute, or some other emergency."

"Don't worry. I'll wait for you." A louder chuckle rang through the phone.

"I'll see you tomorrow."

"Good night, Emma and I am really looking forward to tomorrow."

"Me too," she said before she hung up quickly. Her heart pounded with delight and she jumped up from the bed, excited for the day tomorrow.

She slipped in between the sheets, closed her eyes, and prayed that Thomas's true nature would be revealed. A prayer like that could save her from heartache.

For the first time she felt as though new opportunities were on the horizon. But every time she got too excited and imagined marrying Thomas, she pulled herself back. If things didn't work out she would feel awfully miserable. Better to keep a level head and if things didn't go the way she envisioned, she wouldn't have a great height to fall from.

THE NEXT MORNING AT SEVEN, Emma softly knocked on the neighboring door.

Mrs. Fields opened the door.

"I've got both of them dressed, but I don't have to go anywhere until ten o'clock, Emma. Do you want to take the children down to breakfast by yourself?"

"Sure. I can do that."

"I've packed a bag with spare clothes and hats for both of them. Will you make sure Ben wears his hat? You know how he burns with his fair skin."

"Yes, I know. I always have their hats on them when they're in the sun."

"And what time do you think you'll be back here?"

"I guess around nightfall, maybe six or seven o'clock. What time do you think you'll be home?"

"Quite late, I'd say. It's a six o'clock wedding, but I'm helping my sister to get the bride dressed and all that jazz and then I'd imagine I'll stay on late."

"It sounds like such good fun."

Ben toddled over and wrapped his arms around Emma's leg.

"Good morning, Ben."

Ben didn't reply, but Jemima ran over to her. "Where are we going?" Jemima asked.

"We're going to have breakfast first, and then we going to a farm where you can see animals."

Jemima squealed with excitement.

"Now both of you say goodbye to your mother, and we'll go to get something to eat."

Both children walked over to their mother, and she leaned down and gave them each a kiss and a hug.

"Shall I have them sleep in my room tonight?" Emma asked.

"Yes, that would be good. I was going to ask you about that."

"Have a nice day at the wedding."

"And you have a lovely day too," Mrs. Fields said with a wink.

Emma giggled as she led the children out of the room.

RIGHT ON EIGHT, Emma and the children waited outside the hotel. She saw a buggy down the road and walked to meet it. There were too many cars parked in front of the hotel for him to stop there.

"We're going to that horse there down the road. Do you see it?" she asked the children while pointing at the buggy.

"Yes," said Jemima.

"We're going to ride in the buggy and the horse is going to pull us."

Ben looked interested in what she had to say while Jemima looked pleased and started skipping while jerking on Emma's hand. That sent the backpack on her back off balance while Ben was already growing heavy on her other arm. If she put him down to walk, he'd take forever to get to the buggy and Emma was anxious to see Thomas as soon as she could. She wiggled her shoulders so the backpack, filled with Ben's diapers and spare clothes for both children, would move into a more comfortable position.

When she got close to the buggy, she saw Thomas wasn't there. She looked around, and to her horror, she saw Uncle Joseph walking towards her. She froze to the spot, realizing he hadn't seen her yet. She had two choices. She could walk right past him and in her *Englisch* clothes with two children; he might not even notice her. The other choice was, she could say hello and face what would follow. Then her mind went to the dark side. Had Thomas double-crossed her and told her uncle where to find her?

CHAPTER 19

She was still deciding what to do when Uncle Joseph glanced in her direction and saw her. When he looked just as surprised to see her as she'd been to see him, she figured Thomas hadn't told him anything. Uncle Joseph stopped in his tracks and stared and then his gaze went to the children, and then he slowly walked closer.

"Emma, where have you been?"

"I've been working for someone as a maid and a nanny."

"Your hair is short."

"I cut it."

He nodded. "I can see that."

It was an awkward meeting, both of them seeming to search for words. At that moment, she saw another buggy approaching, and she hoped it was Thomas so she could make a quick getaway.

"Where are you living now?" he asked.

"Pittsburgh. The lady I'm working for is visiting someone here. I'm minding the children for the day."

"Would you visit us while you're here?"

That shocked Emma. "You want me to visit you?"

"Molly has cried many a night wondering how you are. She blames me for you leaving us."

"Oh no. She doesn't, does she? It wasn't her fault, or your fault ... really." But then she could say no more because it kind of was his fault. Still, Emma felt bad that she was a source of unrest between a married couple.

"Where were you off to just now?"

She looked down at the sidewalk beneath her feet. She didn't want to bring Thomas into the conversation, but neither did she want to lie. There had been enough lying and deceiving going on.

"I met Thomas in town yesterday, and he asked me if I would come back and look at his house today. I'm taking the children there." At that precise moment, the buggy passed by them and Thomas was staring at the two of them.

Uncle Joseph caught sight of Thomas's buggy. "And that's him picking you up now?"

"Yes."

"It's good to see you again, Emma. You're always welcome to come back home, and no one will try to make you marry anyone." He shook his head. "I never would've done that if I thought it would make you leave. If I had known you'd be so against it."

Emma knew she couldn't have stood

against it any stronger than she had, but he was kind of apologizing so she didn't want to say anything negative that would make him feel bad. "I haven't left *Gott*," she said to reassure him.

"You know why we keep separate, Emma. If you haven't left Him yet, it's only a matter of time. You become like those you associate with, and if you are not with your brethren you'll be pulled away. Salvation is a narrow path. You've already cut your hair."

"Hair," Ben said, tugging hard on her hair.

Emma let go of Jemima's hand to pull her hair out of Ben's hand because he was starting to hurt her. "Stop it, Ben."

Meanwhile, Jemima took the opportunity to take off at a sprint. Emma ran after her as fast as she could while carrying Ben and weighed down with the heavy backpack. Somehow she caught up with her and grabbed her hand. Then she walked back to her uncle who was still standing there.

"I've always intended to come back to the community," she said to him.

"I hope so. What will I tell your aunt? And Katie?"

He didn't know she'd been writing to Katie under a different name. "I don't know if I'll have time to visit them today or tomorrow. I think we might be leaving tomorrow or the day after that. But next visit, I will come and see you."

He nodded and then tipped his hat slightly back on his head. "It's been nice to see you, Emma. Goodbye. If you manage to make it back to the *haus* this visit, it would make Katie and your aunt very happy."

"Goodbye, *Onkel* Joseph."

She looked around for Thomas and saw him in the distance, walking to meet her, and she couldn't see his buggy anywhere. With Ben on one hip and holding tightly onto Jemima's hand she headed to meet him. Before she reached him, Uncle Joseph's buggy went past her and then a few yards further on, he passed Thomas. Thomas gave him a little wave and then fixed his eyes onto Emma.

"Emma, what happened?"

"I thought the buggy was yours and I walked right up to his buggy, and then I saw that it was him. By then it was too late to turn around."

"I hope you don't think I told him."

She shook her head. "No, I don't. I know you didn't."

"And who do we have here?" he said, now looking at the two children.

"This is Ben, and this is Jemima."

"Hello, Ben." He tickled Ben and then crouched down to Jemima's level. "And how do you do, Jemima?" He put out his hand to shake, and Jemima hit his hand.

Emma laughed. "She only knows how to do a high five."

"High five," he said putting up his hand for her to slap.

When she slapped it, she giggled.

Thomas stood up and his eyes rested on her backpack. "Let me take that for you."

"No, it's okay. It's not far now."

"It is. I could only get a spot to park a fair distance around the corner."

"Okay, thanks." Emma placed Ben down and took off the backpack while she hoped Jemima wouldn't run away again. She'd never done anything like that before.

Thomas slung it over one shoulder and then laughed when he saw Ben reaching his hands up at him to be picked up. He swept Ben up into his arms while leaving Emma to hold Jemima's hand. When giggles rang out of Ben's mouth, Emma knew that Thomas reminded Ben of his father. Ben loved it when his father tossed him in the air and roughhoused with him.

When the children were secured in the

back of the buggy, Thomas set off with Emma sitting beside him.

"It feels strange to be in a buggy again."

"So what else did your uncle say? I hope he's not cross with me for not telling him you were here."

"He didn't seem to be. Anyway I suppose you'll have to talk to him when you see him again at one of the meetings."

"Yes, I'll have a lot of explaining to do."

"Jemima is pleased to be seeing the animals."

"I hope she's not the only one excited about today." He glanced over at her.

CHAPTER 20

"*J*'m looking forward to seeing your place, and you can tell me about your brothers and how they're doing."

"There's nothing to say about them really. They're all married with young families. I'm the odd one out."

"Well, I know how that feels," Emma said. "You must've dated before."

"Must I? Why's that?"

"Well, you've got to be in your late twenties by now."

He shrugged his shoulders. "There's been

one or two quite some time ago, but I never asked either of them to marry me."

Emma giggled.

"And I've asked you twice now," he added smiling at her.

"If I remember correctly, the first time I don't think you asked me at all."

"*Jah,* that's true, but I have apologized for that, haven't I?"

"Yes, you have."

"And now your *onkel* is probably disappointed in both of us," Thomas said.

"That's quite possible," Emma agreed.

Emma felt a little self-conscious not being in Amish clothes. She wore her usual long black skirt and white blouse. There was no covering on her head, and it was odd to be back in an Amish buggy going past familiar farmhouses and feeling so far removed.

"How does it feel to be back home?"

Nowhere had ever felt like home to her after her parents' deaths, but she shook off her depressing thoughts. "It certainly feels odd to be back here. It feels like it was years ago when it wasn't even a whole year yet."

"I was in the process of buying this little house a year ago. I guess that's another reason why it would be perfect that you and I marry."

"It amazes me that we hadn't seen each other for years and you came to a decision like that. It's a very big decision."

"I knew it was right when I saw you again in your uncle's house. When I pulled that silly stunt of pretending not to know you."

Emma said nothing but kept her eyes fixed on the road ahead.

"And I know what feelings you had towards me then. I just hope that you are softening towards me now."

She glanced over at him. "Maybe just a little bit."

"Good." He smiled and then glanced over

his shoulder at the children. "Didn't they sleep last night or something?"

Emma turned around to see that both of the children were nodding off to sleep. "It must be the movement of the buggy and the rhythm of the horse's hooves. They'll be full of energy for the day ahead."

"There's plenty of space to run around."

"Well, that's something they like to do. Especially Jemima lately."

He pulled off the road and traveled a long way down a dirt track. "Is your house up here?" It was a silly question she realized as soon as she said it.

"*Jah.* Since we pulled off the road the land either side is mine."

"Oh, that's a lot of land."

"I guess so. I'm not certain what to do with it yet. I've had a neighbor offer to lease it from me, so maybe I'll do that. I've already got two jobs. I don't need to add farming for the third job or I'd have no time to sleep."

THE AMISH GIRL WHO NEVER BELONGED (AMIS...

Then the house came into view. It was painted red, which stood out against the green landscape. The roof was a charcoal color, and the front door and the frames of the windows were white. And it was two levels just like he'd told her.

"It's red," she said her eyes drawn back to the vibrant color.

"Too bright?" he asked.

"It is a little bright, but it looks nice."

He drove the buggy over to the barn, which was quite close to the house. "I'm afraid we'll have to wake the children up."

"That's okay."

He got out and pulled Ben out of the buggy, and he woke up.

Once Ben was in Emma's arms, he struggled to get down, but she hung onto him tightly. "Don't go anywhere yet, Ben, you can't run around near the horse. And same goes for you, Jemima," Emma said as Thomas placed Jemima next to her. While she was hanging onto the children, they all watched as Thomas unhitched the horse. All the while, Emma was telling the children what he was doing.

Once he was finished rubbing the horse down, he led the horse into the paddock.

"Milk and cookies?" he asked the children.

A grin crossed Ben's face while Jemima answered, "Yes, milk and cookies."

They walked toward the house, and the children let go of her hands, and Jemima ran ahead and then waited by the door. Ben tried to run too, but his chubby legs didn't take him anywhere very quickly. Thomas lifted Ben up the three stairs of the porch and placed him down next to his sister and then he opened the door.

"Don't run inside the house," Emma said to the children.

As soon as she walked in, she was impressed with the cleanliness and the spaciousness of the house.

"Thomas, it's lovely."

There were two dark blue couches facing each other with a small wooden table standing between them. A perfect place to have a quiet cup of coffee of an evening. Close to the couches was a fireplace surrounded by a wooden mantelpiece, and on the top of that was a china clock.

Emma recognized the clock and walked toward it. "This was your mother's?"

"Yes, she gave it to me before she died. My father gave it to her on their wedding day."

Emma walked closer to the clock that she hadn't seen in years. Memories of the happy Esh household flooded through her mind. "They were happy days. The only happy days of my childhood after my mother and father died."

"Is that right?"

Emma was too choked up and couldn't

speak. She turned around and gave him a nod.

"I didn't know. I thought they would've been your worst days, with all that hard work."

Emma sighed. "My grandmother was a very hard and strict woman. Unhappy. I think I only ever saw her smile twice. One time when she was speaking about my grandfather, and I don't remember why she smiled the other time, but I took notice of it." Emma looked around at the walls. "This was an old house, you say?"

"*Jah.* It was built from solid logs and was strong enough for me to put another level on. I had my brothers' help, of course."

"You did it all yourselves?"

He shook his head. "We had a lot of help."

That made sense. The community always rallied around and helped people who were building, or rebuilding.

"I hoped you'd like it. I was cleaning it all

night and hardly had any sleep." He chuckled. "I won't show you upstairs. There are just bedrooms and a small bathroom. The bathroom downstairs is just through that door there." He pointed to a doorway near the stairs.

"Well, you've done a marvelous job."

"*Denke.*"

"Where are the cookies and milk?" Jemima asked.

"In the kitchen. It's this way." They followed him into the kitchen.

"I think that's the longest sentence Jemima has ever said."

Thomas chuckled. "She must be hungry."

"She's always hungry for cookies," Emma said.

The kitchen was old-fashioned with an uneven floor covered with ugly gray linoleum. The stove was in a large bricked area that looked like an old fireplace. In front of the window was the sink.

"What a beautiful view you have out the window," Emma said.

"And that is a very subtle way of saying that you don't like my kitchen."

Emma giggled. "I don't mean that at all."

"It's on my list of things I have to do next."

Emma sat down at the kitchen table and put Jemima on a chair next to her while she placed Ben on her lap.

"I gather you don't want milk, Emma?" Thomas asked.

"No thanks."

"I've got orange juice or I can make you *kaffe*."

"Coffee sounds good, thanks."

He placed cookies on the table and poured out two cups of milk for the children.

"Have some milk first before you eat the cookies," Emma told the children, seeing their eyes fixed on the chocolate chip cookies. Emma held the cup while Thomas watched that Ben took a couple of mouthfuls, and Jemima was now capable of holding a glass by herself.

"Now can I have a cookie?" Jemima asked when she had carefully set her glass back down on the table.

"Yes, you can."

"Thank you."

"You're very polite, Jemima," Thomas said as he filled the kettle with water. Jemima giggled in response to the compliment.

When both children were eating their cookies the crumbs were flying everywhere.

"I'm afraid we're creating a mess," Emma said.

"Don't worry about that."

"It must be nice living out here. I've missed the peace and quiet of being on a farm. It's busy where I've been living. There are always cars. Even at night I can hear cars in the distance when I'm sleeping, and everything is so fast-paced all the time."

"Yes, I like the silence and the big wide open spaces. You'll never catch me living in the city."

"Can we see the animals?" Jemima asked.

"When you finish your cookies and your milk, and when Emma and I finish our coffee," Thomas said smiling at Jemima.

He had a kind way of speaking to the children. He was firm, and yet kind.

CHAPTER 21

Thomas sipped his coffee and looked at the beautiful woman across from him. He imagined what it would be like if these children were theirs and this was his family. If he could persuade Emma to marry him, his life would be complete.

Emma glanced up at him when she took a sip of her coffee and gave him a little smile. It seemed she was embarrassed that he was looking at her. But why wouldn't he look at her? She was everything a man would want in a woman—kind and goodhearted, smart and a bit spunky, and it didn't hurt that she was nice to look at, too.

Emma didn't have a deceptive bone in her body and it was no wonder that she had shied away from him a year ago in her uncle's house.

He'd made terrible choices in his life and he'd confessed his wrongdoing. Emma might never forgive him, though, or forget the way he had been as a young man. As she spoke softly to the children instructing them on their manners, he knew she would be a wonderful mother. The best thing was that his mother had loved her before she died. He knew he had his mother's approval and that was something that meant a great deal to him.

"What are you smiling at?" Emma asked when she looked up at him.

"I'm smiling because I remember you as a young girl doing so much work all by yourself. My brothers and I always made sure we helped you wherever we could."

"Yes, and that was something I appreciated. Believe me, if it weren't for all of you being so kind, my life there could've been very bad."

"Who would've thought we'd be here now, all these years later?"

"Not me," she said.

The children had just finished their second cookies.

"I don't think they have to drink all that milk today, do they?" he asked.

"Probably not. They only finished breakfast a little while ago."

He stood up and gathered up the dishes and put them in the sink. "I'll wash these later." He clapped his hands. "Is everyone ready to go outside?"

The children had a lovely time at the farm. They played with the hens and their chicks, and got to pat the horses, and then Jemima had a ride on one of the horses while Emma held onto her. Just before it was time to head back, they fed the ducks during the picnic Thomas had made for them to eat by the river.

198

CHAPTER 22

wo very tired children had again fallen asleep in the buggy, and Emma had carried Ben up to the hotel room while Thomas carried Jemima.

Thomas was quick to say goodnight and then she was alone. Now that the children were in bed, she had time to reflect on the day and it hadn't escaped her how patient and kind Thomas was with the children. She could tell it wasn't an act, he was genuine.

The chilly weather had been replaced by a warm clear night. She looked across the room at the sleeping children and thought about her future. Was this what she wanted to do forever, look after someone else's home and children?

The hours passed by slowly, but her mind never shied away from Thomas and the happenings of the day.

Giving up on trying to stop thinking about Thomas, she decided to get some sleep, but even that proved to be difficult. For what felt like hours, she lay there, clenching her eyes tightly with the intentions of ridding her mind of thoughts of him. Darkness seeped in soon enough, but only so the dreams could take over.

A desolate, burning field in the middle of nowhere lay before Emma's eyes now. She lifted her soiled body from the trampled grass, moaning in agony as she tried to figure out where she was. Then, she saw him: the lecherous, evil person with bad intentions. He was walking toward her with a large sword in hand as a metal helmet hid most of his face. Then, he slowly raised the sword in both hands, holding it tightly, and then he struck.

To her surprise however, the blade passed by, cutting the air by her right shoulder missing it by a matter of inches. When she turned around, she noticed that he had just slain a vicious beast, one that'd had her in its sights without her even realizing it was there.

"Emma, are you okay?" he asked. "Emma!"

Just then, Emma opened her eyes to see Mrs. Fields hovering above her.

"I'm sorry, I didn't want to wake you but you were moaning and looked distressed. I just came to check on the children."

Emma sat up. "I was having a bad dream. I'm glad you woke me. How was your night?" she asked Mrs. Fields while rubbing her eyes.

"Oh, it was so good. Did they go to sleep quickly?"

"Yes they did."

"The wedding was wonderful." Mrs. Fields sat on the edge of her bed. "And this lovely stole; where on earth did you find it? I haven't seen quality like this in some time."

"There's this wonderful little store just off the main street," Emma said, her thoughts immediately focusing on Thomas once more. *Oh no, not again!*

"At the wedding there was this one single man and all the women were clamoring to talk with him. He was handsome and wealthy. You should've come there to the reception to meet him."

Emma giggled. "I don't know that I'm the marrying kind." A year ago, she was running away from Thomas, and now she wasn't sure why she'd run without getting to know him and giving him a chance.

Mrs. Fields stood up. "I should let you get back to sleep. Sorry to wake you."

"It's fine," Emma said as she slid back lower under the covers. "Oh, Mrs. Fields."

"Yes?"

"Thomas wants me to meet him tomorrow. Would that be okay?"

"Ah, so that's his name?"

Emma nodded.

"Take all the time you want." Mrs. Fields grinned and then turned off the light before she closed the door.

As Emma closed her eyes she thought again about Thomas. The same question as always lingered in her mind—what if he hadn't really changed? She had seen him smoking in the alley, but many of the Amish men had a smoke every now and again. She knew she shouldn't let that one incident color her impression of him.

THE DAY BEFORE, Thomas had told her he wanted to meet to discuss where things would go from there. The way Emma saw things, the only thing she could do was write to him. Or speak on the phone if he chose to call. It was too soon for anything else.

When she walked back into the same café where they'd met once before, he was there already. It made Emma feel happy inside to know how important she was to someone.

"You look lovely, as always," he said.

Emma sat across from him. "Thank you," she said, her cheeks warming at the mention of her appearance.

When the waitress came over he ordered for both of them, the same as they'd had the first time they were there. "Okay, with you?" he quickly asked Emma before the waitress left.

"Yes. That's fine."

"I have some things to get off my chest," he said.

"I'm listening."

Emma watched as he paused, covering his face with both hands. That's how he sat for the next few minutes, but when his fingers slowly fell to reveal red-rimmed eyes, he spoke once more.

"I didn't know what to do or who would want to marry someone like me, but then I remembered you. Some of the many memories that I cherished with my mother involved her words of you. Back when you worked for her during her illnesses, you imprinted upon her greatly. She used to tell me that I should always aim to marry someone like Emma; someone sweet, gentle, caring, and beautiful. And most importantly, someone with a good heart, since they were the toughest to find. She even joked about how finding another girl with all of those traits was going to be impossible, but I just laughed it off every time. I guess she was correct, though," Thomas said, now smiling at her.

Emma looked back at him, her stomach fluttering in ways it never had before. "It's not how she talked about you to me." Back then she was only a girl and it didn't make sense that Mrs. Esh would look so far ahead into the future. Besides, she used to despair of what would become of him.

"Don't look so confused, Emma. We both want the same thing, don't we?"

"I guess we do."

"I'm so glad I waited for you that day in the city." He chuckled. "Although, I could've done without you seeing me with a smoke in my hand."

"Wait. What do you mean 'waited for me?'"

He looked away.

"No more lies, Thomas. Did someone tell you where I'd be that day I saw you in the alley?"

Blowing out a deep breath, he slowly nodded.

"Tell me it wasn't Katie."

"It was, but don't be mad with her. I forced her to tell me."

Emma jumped to her feet. The closest people in the world to her had both lied to her and deceived her. She marched out of the café. She'd get on the first train back to Pittsburgh in the morning.

"Wait, Emma."

He touched her arm when he caught up with her and she pulled away from him. Then he jumped in front of her forcing her to stop.

"There's nothing you can say, Thomas. The two people I trusted the most... well, I so wanted to trust you, but I definitely trusted Katie and she deceived me." Emma stepped past him with a wide step to the side and hurried down the street.

CHAPTER 23

*T*homas watched her run from him. He loved her, and now he'd lost her, just when he was sure her barriers were coming down. He thought he could win every situation with trickery and planning. He headed back to the café where he'd left his coat over the chair. Seeing the food still there, he slumped down into the chair and was forced to reexamine his life.

He knew how he wanted his life to turn out—marry a good woman and have loads of children and a happy home. That's what all men wanted, so why was he different from his brothers? They'd been married for years and he'd stayed single. Befriending Katie and winning her to his cause had seemed a clever thing to do and now the very action that brought him and Emma together might be the same action that tore them apart.

Staring at the grain in the wooden table-top, he told himself his actions were horrible. He'd lied about his mother telling him Emma was a good woman for him. It had been nothing but lies and Emma knew it too —he could tell by the look on her face.

Emma deserved better, a lot better man than he was. He'd first hurt her when he turned up at her uncle's house, and again just now. He would not allow there to be a third time.

"Is your friend coming back?" the waitress asked.

"Um, no. Would you have pen and paper that I could borrow?"

"Yes. I think so."

She came back a few minutes later with two sheets of copier paper and a pen. The only thing, and the right thing to do, was write a letter of confession to Emma and then he'd leave her alone.

The words flowed onto the paper. He confessed that he was always trying to manipulate life to go his way, and he'd been like that as a child and his actions worsened when he was a teenager.

He begged her not to be mad at Katie for revealing that she was visiting Lancaster and was staying at that hotel. It was he who had deceived Katie into believing it was in Emma's best interests, and he had believed it was, back then. The next big confession was that his mother had never said anything about the two of them being good for each other. It was a trick to gain her trust. Thomas had to stop himself from adding that his mother would've been delighted if Emma had married one of her sons. No! He would not bring his mother into it any further. It was bad enough that he'd lied.

He ended the letter with a goodbye and told Emma that she deserved someone good, someone who matched her integrity and honesty. It had been a struggle for him to stay on the narrow path over the years, he told her as well.

There was so much more he wanted to say, but the restaurant worker had only given him two sheets of paper. He folded them and put them into his pocket.

After he paid for the meal, he headed off to slip the note under her hotel door. Then he'd disappear from her life. Tonight in his home, he'd tell God he was sorry and he'd confess all the ways he'd tried to manipulate things to make Emma his wife. He'd always seen his scheming mind as being an advantage, but now he saw it was the opposite.

EMMA SAT in her hotel room, unhappy about Thomas and his deception. She was convinced that he loved her and he probably would've been a good husband to her, but it would bother her always never knowing if she could believe his words. Trust was a huge thing in a marriage.

If only she'd never learned the truth about Katie plotting with a man behind her back. Ignorance of the situation would've been far better. Now she felt even more alone than she had when she'd lived with her severe grandmother.

When Emma heard a rustle near the door, she looked over to see some paper appear under the door. She walked over and picked up the note. When she looked through the peephole, she saw Thomas walking away.

She sat down on the couch and read what she thought would be an apology of sorts.

There was one confession after another instead, and it ended with a goodbye.

Emma wiped a tear from her eye. She'd had a timely escape from him, but it scared her that she was ready to accept a proposal from him if he'd asked again. At least he'd been man enough to admit his wrongs.

After she stood up and pushed the note into the bottom of her suitcase, she went to find out from Mrs. Fields if they were leaving in the morning.

EMMA KNOCKED on Mrs. Fields's door. She opened the door and smiled. "There you are. The children are asleep now. Come in." She stepped aside to let her in the room. "Is everything all right? You look dreadful."

"Things didn't go as planned with Thomas."

"Oh, I'm sorry to hear that."

"Are we going back home tomorrow?"

"Yes, we can if you want to do that."

"I'd like that."

"I was only going to stay an extra day if you wanted to spend some more time with your friends."

Emma shook her head. "No, I'd rather go, if that's okay."

"I'll call down to reception and tell them we're booking out in the morning."

Emma nodded while trying to stop herself from crying.

"Take the rest of the night off. I know you always help with the bathing and with the feeding of the children, but take some time for yourself."

Emma sniffed. "Would that be all right?"

"More than all right."

"Thank you." Emma opened the door and went back to her own room. She fished Thomas's letter out of her bag and read it one more time. She wished she had listened to her inner promptings from the beginning.

She had been suspicious that he hadn't changed, and he'd proved she was right.

AFTER THEY GOT HOME the next day, Emma was cooking the evening meal for the children when the phone rang. Mrs. Fields was nowhere about so Emma answered it. "Hello."

"Emma, this is Katie."

That was the last person she wanted to hear from. Katie had deceived her in the worst possible way.

"Before you say anything, Thomas told me what happened. I know you must hate me right now."

"I don't hate you," Emma said. And it was true; she didn't hate her. She just felt numb toward her.

"I can tell by your voice you're angry with me."

"You let me down, Katie. That's all I've got to say."

She heard Katie sob. "I'm sorry. Will you ever forgive me?"

"I must go. I am cooking the children's dinner."

And then Katie wailed. "Don't be like this, Emma."

"It's true. I have to feed the children." Emma hung up and then realized she hadn't said goodbye. But it was most likely better that way. Emma needed a clean break from everybody who had hurt her.

CHAPTER 24

A year passed and every week she had gotten a letter from Katie, and still she hadn't been able to bring herself to write back even though she had read every one of those letters.

When she got a letter from Katie in a purple envelope, her curiosity was raised. Normally she read the letters at night, but not this one. She ripped it open and read it as soon as she got it out of the mailbox.

Katie wrote that she was getting married

and she wanted Emma to be at the wedding. Tears rolled down Emma's face when she remembered how close they used to be. She'd always assumed she'd be an attendant at Katie's wedding and now Katie was getting married without her.

Emma sniffed back her tears and read further that she was marrying Thomas … Emma held her heart. No, she couldn't be marrying *her* Thomas. She read on that she was marrying Thomas Hersler. Emma didn't know a Thomas Hersler, but she was happy for Katie. Relief washed over her body, and she folded the letter up and put it in her pocket. She'd read it more thoroughly later that night in the privacy of her own bedroom. Right now, the children needed her attention.

Throughout the day, her reaction to thinking that her cousin was marrying Thomas Esh bothered her. In her heart, she still liked him even though she knew he had a great many problems. If she had married Thomas those problems would sooner or later become her problems. She wanted marriage to bring her a life full of happiness, not a life full of problems and torment.

When she reread the letter that night, she found out that the wedding was in one month's time. Although she was still hurt by Katie's actions, she would attend her wedding to honor the good times they'd had together.

She pulled stationary out of her drawer and for the first time since she'd been back, she wrote a letter to Katie telling her that she would be at the wedding. Mrs. Fields would give her the time off, she knew that for certain.

THOMAS GOT DRESSED in his best suit for Katie and Thomas Hersler's wedding. He wondered again if Emma was going to be there. He hadn't had an opportunity to ask Katie these past weeks leading up to the wedding but knowing that Emma had not responded to any of Katie's letters, Thomas figured she wouldn't come to the wedding either.

In the past several months he'd acted with integrity in all his dealings and associations with people. He no longer took delight in trying to sway people or situations to his advantage. What had happened with Emma had changed him for the better, but he wished it hadn't taken losing Emma to make him face himself head on.

Emma hadn't responded to the letter that he had slipped under that hotel door. If she'd forgiven him surely she would've sent him back a note or at least a message through Katie. It seemed as though both Katie and he had lost Emma. He was sorry he had come between the cousins by persuading Katie the way that he had.

He tied his bowtie and then placed his hat on his head before he went to hitch his horse to the buggy.

CHAPTER 25

*E*mma found a reasonably priced B&B not far from Katie's house, which was where the wedding would take place. It certainly would feel odd, being back there again, coming face-to-face with all the people she'd run away from. And then there was the bishop. She knew he would be disappointed in her as well. Then she reminded herself that it was Katie she was going there for and no one else.

She wondered what had become of Thomas Esh. Maybe he was married by now.

Katie hadn't mentioned it in any of her letters but neither had she said anything at all about Thomas. Her letters had been half filled with news and half filled with apologies and urging Emma to write back to her. It was also odd, she thought, that Katie had not mentioned having a special man in her life. Surely her uncle wouldn't have tried his hand at matching two people together again, seeing that it had worked so badly last time.

The wedding was at ten in the morning and she had not told Katie she was going to turn up. The letter... Yes, she'd written it, but it never made it to the mailbox. She wanted to talk to Katie alone before the wedding so she had a taxi take her to the house at nine thirty. That would give her plenty of time to talk to her uncle and aunt and then speak to Katie in private.

When the taxi approached the house, she could see there were already buggies lined in a row.

She kept her head down and walked to the door and knocked on it. That felt strange; she had never knocked on that door before. Her aunt opened it and screeched with delight, slapping her hand over her mouth and crying.

"Come here," Aunt Molly said, squeezing her into a tight hug. "I'm so glad you've come. Katie didn't say that you answered her."

Emma shook her head. "I didn't send a reply, I'm sorry. I hope it's alright that I'm here."

"We're so glad you came." She yelled over her shoulder to Joseph while she dragged Emma into the kitchen.

Uncle Joseph was eating at the kitchen table and he stood up when he saw her. Emma could tell by his face that he was pleased to see her.

"Hello, *Onkel* Joseph."

"Hello. I'm so glad you've come, Emma,

so happy that you've come."

"Is Katie upstairs?"

"*Jah.* Go up and see her."

Emma turned and ran up the stairs taking them two by two and then she quietly knocked on Katie's door.

The door opened and Katie stood there in a mid-blue dress that had to be her wedding dress.

Katie took a step back and her face went white. "You came."

"Yes."

Katie leaped forward and wrapped her arms around her and gave her a hug nearly as tight as the one her mother had given her.

"Thank you for coming. I didn't know if I was writing to the wrong address or if you just didn't write back to me. So I kept writing, figuring out I'd find out one way or another soon enough."

"Something stopped me from writing. I mean, I wrote but I didn't…"

Katie stepped back. "Stubbornness stopped you, that's what."

Emma shrugged her shoulders. "Let's not talk about all that today. You're getting married and this is an exciting day. I want to be here for you."

When they heard a buggy coming, Katie looked out the window. "That's my attendants."

Emma crossed over to the window to find out who her attendants were.

"I don't know them."

"That's true. They moved here from Ohio six months ago. They are sisters, Fannie and Gabby."

"I should wait downstairs then, and let you girls get ready."

"I'm so happy you're here, Emma. Where are you staying?"

"I'm staying at a B&B close to here."

"When do you have to go back?"

"In a couple of days."

Katie's lips turned down at the corners. "Thomas and I are leaving tomorrow morning."

"I haven't even met him yet."

"You'll like him. He is Fannie and Gabby's older brother."

"I'll see you after you're an old married lady," Emma joked.

"I'm so glad you're here." Katie hugged Emma once again.

Emma went downstairs and while people filed through the doors the bishop looked over and caught her eye and gave her a polite nod and a smile. Seeing him wasn't as bad as she'd thought it would be. When the room was filled with people sitting on the wooden benches that had been brought into the house especially for the wedding, Emma saw Thomas Esh squeeze his way into the door. She looked away hoping he wouldn't see her. When she looked back again she saw he'd taken a seat up front in the second row.

There was a nervous looking man shifting his weight from one foot to the other as he stood at the bottom of the stairs. Emma guessed that he was the groom.

Emma suddenly broke out in a sweat and felt she couldn't breathe. She walked out to get some fresh air. It would be a few minutes before everything started and then she could slip back inside and no one would notice that she had been gone.

CHAPTER 26

Thomas couldn't believe his eyes when he saw that Emma was there. That had to be God giving him a second chance. No, a third chance. He glanced around to have another look at her to make sure he hadn't imagined it, but when he did, he saw her disappearing out through the kitchen and heading left. He remembered that the back door was to the left. She was heading outside, and this might be his only opportunity to speak to her alone.

He sent up a silent prayer for God to help them if this was meant to be.

When he walked out the front door and around to the back of the house he saw Emma standing with her back to him.

"Emma."

She turned around to face him and he couldn't help but smile.

"Hello, Thomas. How have you been?"

Hearing a friendly response and the fact that she wasn't screaming at him and warning him to keep away, he stepped forward. "I've been fine, and you?"

"Good."

"I guess you got my letter that I slipped under the door of the hotel room?"

She nodded. "That was a long time ago."

He stared at her and didn't know what to say. He wanted to tell her he'd changed but he told her once before that he'd changed when he hadn't. What would make her believe him this time, and did he deserve to be believed by her?

"I saw you were heading out the back and I took this opportunity to have a private word with you." He gave a little chuckle. "You know how these weddings can be."

"I do."

"Are you married?" he asked.

She laughed and looked down at the ground. "No, I'm not." She looked up at him. "Are you?"

"No, I'm not. I've been waiting for you to come back to me."

She laughed and put a hand up. "Don't start again, Thomas."

He had to give this one more shot. "Emma, I know I've got a bad track record and you deserve someone so much better but I have changed. You can ask anybody. Two of my brothers are here today and you can ask them."

Her face brightened. "Your brothers are here. I'd like to see them again."

"Forget them. My point is you can ask anybody—the bishop for instance. I unburdened my heart to him when you left and told him what a manipulating scheming person I was and he prayed with me for God's help to change. And I have changed." He put out his hand. "I'll take you to the bishop right now and I'll ask him in front of you."

"No, we can't do that. We'll ruin the wedding."

"How about after the wedding?"

"You're very persistent."

"That's because I like you, Emma. I like you a lot. And don't you miss the community?"

"I do. I belong back in the community. I know that now; that's why I had to come outside and get some fresh air. I need to return and recommit my life to God and start all over again."

"You don't know how pleased that makes me. We should probably go inside now, though, or we'll miss your cousin's wedding."

Together, they walked through the back door.

EMMA SAT down in her seat at the back while Thomas made his way to the front of the room to sit back where he'd been, in the second row. They'd come back at just the right time because now Katie was walking down the stairs and all eyes were on her. She looked beautiful in her carefully sewn blue dress, with the white organza prayer *kapp* and apron. The two attendants followed her down the stairs, both dressed in a darker shade of blue.

Katie met her groom at the bottom of the

stairs and together they walked to the front of the room to stand in front of the bishop.

The rest was a blur to Emma; she was thinking of what she would say to Mrs. Fields about leaving her employment. What about Ben and Jemima? She'd miss seeing them grow up. Ben was starting to speak a lot and even recognize some words in the books she read to him and his sister. Then she reminded herself again; she could get married and raise her own children if God willed it.

The next step was to talk to the bishop and tell him of her plans.

During the meal after the ceremony was when she saw the bishop alone, as he was helping himself to food at the desserts table.

"Hello, Bishop John."

He turned to look at her with a smile on his face. "Hello. It's good to see you back here, Emma."

She rubbed her forehead wondering how

to start the conversation. "I would like to return to the community."

He raised his eyebrows slightly. "That's *wunderbaar* news."

Emma was relieved he was pleased. She hadn't been baptized so she wouldn't have been shunned for choosing to leave the community. "I thought I could rent a house somewhere nearby as soon as I go back home and tell my employer I'm leaving. I would have to give her a few weeks notice to give her time to find someone else."

"What's this about you leasing a *haus?*"

"I'd like to live alone in my own place."

"And you can later on, but when you first come back here — in those first few months — it's best to live with a family."

Emma was through with living with other people and never having a place of her own. Never fitting in. If she had her own house she'd only have herself to worry about. "I'd rather live in my own place. I've never really done that and I think at my age it's good that I live by myself."

He shook his head. "The best thing that you could do is live back here with Joseph and Molly."

Emma felt a pain in the pit of her stomach. "If I come back here, I will feel like I'm going backward instead of forward."

"Emma, sometimes in life we have to retrace our steps and take two paces back before we can take two paces forward. Do you see what I mean?"

Emma thought about it for a moment. He was saying amends needed to be made, she thought. "I'd really rather not."

"It's either that or another family."

"If they are my only two choices I would prefer to move back here. How long would that be for?"

"Eight weeks."

Emma felt like a load had been lifted off

her shoulders. Eight weeks was not long at all. "I could do that," she said with a smile.

The bishop glanced around. "And might I asked what prompted this change of heart, or *who* prompted this change of heart?" He didn't let her get a word in before he continued, "Because if you've got your eyes on a particular young man, I must insist that the same amount of time would have to apply before an engagement takes place, and of course you'd want to be baptized?"

"*Jah,* I do." Emma knew he was referring to Thomas when he mentioned a young man. "I've got nothing like that on my mind—about a man, believe me."

"I know you've had a difficult time of things in your life, Emma, but don't close your heart off. None of us is perfect, not even you."

Emma was a little taken aback. What had he heard about her? Did he mean she wasn't perfect because she'd left the community? Or she just wasn't perfect in general, because she knew no one was, but it was a weird thing for him to say.

"I know I'm not perfect," she expressed in a small voice but now he was too busy heaping various portions of desserts on his plate to hear.

When he straightened up he looked back at her. "How about we go and find your *Onkel* Joseph and tell him the good news?"

"I hope he'll think it's good news."

"Of course he will, and so will Molly. They'll be delighted to have you back. They were dreading having an empty home."

"I hope you're right." Emma followed the bishop, who was making his way to the table where Molly and Joseph sat.

242

CHAPTER 27

Things had gone fairly smoothly for Emma with her transition back into the community. It was weird living in her aunt and uncle's house without her cousin there. Katie and her new husband lived close by, and she saw them nearly every day. The rift between the two of them had been mended. Emma knew how persuasive Thomas Esh could be, and she couldn't blame Katie for having been swayed. Besides, Katie would've thought she was doing it for Emma's own good.

In the several weeks that Emma had been back in the community, Thomas had stayed at a respectful distance. Emma had kept her eyes on him, watching all the while to see if he had changed. And she believed that he had. Now she was willing to put the past behind them, and she wondered if Thomas still held feelings for her like he once had. She sincerely hoped so.

Her aunt and uncle had told her she could stay there as long as she wanted, but she was ready to leave. Either to move to live in a house by herself, or if God willed it, to marry Thomas and begin a life together with him.

Knowing Thomas would be home this particular Saturday afternoon, she baked an apple pie and borrowed her uncle's buggy to deliver it to him. That's what the single ladies did to impress the men they had interest in. If he saw that she'd brought him a pie it would be a sign that she was now ready to consider him as a potential husband.

. . .

SHE KNOCKED on his door and then he came to the door with a hammer in his hand. "Oh, I didn't hear a buggy."

"I heard the hammering," she said with a laugh. "Here, I've brought you a pie."

His gaze dropped to the checkered tea towel covering the pie that she held out with both hands. "For me?"

"*Jah,* just for you."

"That is so lovely of you." He looked down at the dust on his hands and wiped them on the sides of his pants before he took the pie from her.

A giggle escaped her lips. "I hope I haven't interrupted your repairs."

He chuckled as he corrected her. "Renovations, and you haven't. Why don't I make us each a cup of *kaffe* and we can sit on the porch and have a piece of this pie?"

"Okay."

"You sit down. I won't be long."

She sat on a porch chair and looked over the yard and to the river beyond it. It certainly was a beautiful spot. It wasn't as close to town as her uncle and aunt's house, but that meant it was quieter.

"There, I've got the water heating and now my hands are clean." He cleared his throat. "Now in the interests of me being totally honest and upfront, I have to tell you that I talked to the bishop about you."

That pleased Emma. "What did you say?"

"I asked if I had to wait to ask you out and he said I'd have to wait and he said he'd told you the same."

Emma smiled. "I think that amount of time has passed."

"Are you saying what I think you're saying?"

Nodding, she said, "I am."

"So you'd be willing to go on a buggy ride with me or go on a date sometime soon?"

"I'd like that." Things were going exactly as she had hoped they'd go.

"I should've been honest like this a long time ago."

"*Jah*, you should have."

Thomas leaned forward, placing his hand palm-side up on the table. He smiled at her, glancing down at his hand. Emma let her hand slowly fall into his. With a soft grasp, he held it and looked deep into her eyes.

"Emma Schwartz, will you marry me?"

That came as a surprise. She didn't think he'd ask so soon.

He immediately pulled his hand away. "I'm sorry. I can wait. I'm so stupid. You would think I would've learned patience by now."

She reached for his hand and took hold of it, and he grasped her hand in both of his.

Emma looked into his sincere, dark eyes and tears came to hers. For the first time that she could remember, she felt that she was truly home. That she belonged somewhere. *"Jah,* I'll marry you, Thomas Esh."

A smile brightened his face, and then he shook his head. "That makes me the happiest man alive. If I wasn't so stupid, I could've saved us both a lot of time. It's taken us so long to get to this day."

"Let's not look back. We can't change our past, either one of us, but we can make a good future together."

"I like the sound of that. You know what else?"

"What?"

"Our birthday is in six weeks' time. Let's get married on that day. We'll turn what was always a bad day for the both of us into a very *gut* day."

Sniffing and trying not to let the tears fall from her eyes, she remembered her seventh birthday and then all the bad happenings nearly every birthday after that. "I'd like that.

We'd be really putting the past behind us then."

"I'll talk to the bishop tomorrow."

Emma nodded.

"I wonder what *Mamm* would think about us marrying. She'd be so pleased. I'm excited for our future. I've never been settled since *Mamm* died."

"*Jah,* but she'd be more pleased that you've changed your ways. She was always so worried about you."

He nodded and Emma could see tears brimming in his eyes as well. He pulled her close to him and whispered in her ear. "*Denke* for giving me another chance, Emma."

"*Denke* for waiting for me to give you one."

"I would've waited forever, but I'm happy I didn't have to," he said before he placed a soft kiss on her forehead.

· · ·

EMMA SCHWARTZ and Thomas Esh were married on their joint birthday, the fifth of September. At the wedding ceremony, Bishop John gave a short sermon about how God turns mourning into dancing. Psalm 30: 11. And that's just what God had done for Emma and Thomas.

Thou hast turned for me my mourning into dancing: thou hast put off my sackcloth, and girded me with gladness;
Psalm 30:11

AMISH MISFITS

Book 7 My Brother's Keeper

Book 8 The Amish Marriage Pact

ALL BOOK SERIES

Amish Maids Trilogy

Amish Love Blooms

Amish Misfits

The Amish Bonnet Sisters

Amish Women of Pleasant Valley

Ettie Smith Amish Mysteries

Amish Secret Widows' Society

Expectant Amish Widows

Seven Amish Bachelors

Amish Foster Girls

Amish Brides

Amish Romance Secrets

Amish Twin Hearts

Amish Wedding Season

Amish Baby Collection

Gretel Koch Jewel Thief

ABOUT SAMANTHA PRICE

USA Today Bestselling author, Samantha Price, wrote stories from a young age, but it wasn't until later in life that she took up writing full time. Formally an artist, she exchanged her paintbrush for the computer and, many best-selling book series later, has never looked back.

Samantha is happiest on her computer lost in the world of her characters. She is best known for the Ettie Smith Amish Mysteries series and the Expectant Amish Widows series.

www.SamanthaPriceAuthor.com

Samantha loves to hear from her readers.
Connect with her at:
samantha@samanthapriceauthor.com
www.facebook.com/SamanthaPriceAuthor
Follow Samantha Price on BookBub
Twitter @ AmishRomance
Instagram - SamanthaPriceAuthor

Made in the USA
Monee, IL
02 August 2021